# Stooping, Van sniffed. "Mmm… that scent suits you."

As they moved on, Anny noticed that French women of all ages, from teenage girls to women with matronly figures, looked with interest at the man strolling beside her.

She basked in the pleasure of knowing that this evening she looked like other girls of seventeen and was out for the evening with a man who might be considered a bit too old for her now, but wouldn't always be. Each year the age gap between them would become less important. She just had to pray that he wouldn't fall in love with anyone else before she was ready for love. Seventeen was too young. She knew that. But eighteen was officially grown-up, and nineteen was old enough for anything…even marriage.

Dear Reader,

If the name of one of the people in this story rings a bell, it's because you have met her before...as a child in one of my longer books, *Summer's Awakening*, published by Worldwide in 1984.

The hero of that story was a computer tycoon, as is the hero of this one. Remembering my introduction to the exciting world of computers during a winter in America in the early eighties, I also remembered the people in *Summer's Awakening* and the letters from readers suggesting a sequel.

This book is not a sequel, but it answers some of the questions about what happened to Emily.

*Anne Weale*

# The Impatient Virgin
## Anne Weale

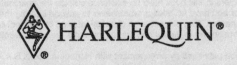

**HARLEQUIN®**

TORONTO • NEW YORK • LONDON
AMSTERDAM • PARIS • SYDNEY • HAMBURG
STOCKHOLM • ATHENS • TOKYO • MILAN • MADRID
PRAGUE • WARSAW • BUDAPEST • AUCKLAND

ISBN 0-373-17399-7

THE IMPATIENT VIRGIN

First North American Publication 1998.

Copyright © 1998 by Anne Weale.

# CHAPTER ONE

THEY were walking briskly across the park, a tall, fair-haired couple who might have been brother and sister, when Jon reached for her hand and laced his fingers through hers.

Until that moment, Anny had been relaxed and care-free, one of the many Londoners enjoying the sunshine in Hyde Park on a spring afternoon after a long cold winter. As his fingers tightened, intuition told her the gesture was more than a friendly impulse.

She had thought that if, some time in the future, he proposed to her, it would be at a secluded table in a quiet restaurant after a candle-lit dinner. Jon was that kind of man: romantic, conventional, predictable but also totally reliable. Everyone who knew him liked him. But even though they had known each other for some time, she was still uncertain how she would answer him, if and when the time came.

Now, in quite different circumstances from the way she had imagined, she sensed that any second now he was going to pop the question.

They had left the path and were cutting across the grass in the direction of the lake. There was nobody near them. He drew her to a halt, released her fingers and took her face between his hands. Big hands, but always gentle.

Her hair tossed about by the breeze which had rosied her winter-pale cheeks, Anny looked into his eyes and longed to say, 'No, Jon...not yet. I'm not ready.' At the same time she shrank from hurting him.

As he opened his mouth to speak, her cellphone

started to ring in the pocket of her red fleece squall jacket.

Jon growled something which, translated, would probably be a taboo word in English. He had learnt to speak Turkish for his work as a plant conservationist, and had smatterings of other languages. She had never heard him swear in his own. He had a placid temperament. It took a lot to rile him.

'I'll say I'm busy.' She took the telephone out of her pocket and extended the aerial. 'Hello?'

'Greg here…got a job for you.' The caller was the editor of the colour magazine of a Sunday newspaper. 'All the morning flights from Gatwick and Heathrow are booked solid, so you'll have to fly from Stansted. The flight number…'

Anny had been a journalist in London for five years. She never went anywhere without a pencil and small pad in her pocket. Holding the phone to her ear with her shoulder, she wrote down the details. *Air UK Flight 910 Business Class 15 April 1120 hours Destination Nice.*

Nice, on the Bay of Angels, on the French Riviera. She could see it in her mind's eye. Fountains sparkling in the sun. Palm trees and beds of green grass dividing the three lanes of traffic along the Promenade des Anglais, named after the English who had invented the concept of wintering in the sun. A blue sea lapping the beach and, nearby, in the old quarter, the stalls of the flower market bright with fluffy golden mimosa, symbol of the mild climate. A city she had known well, but would never willingly go back to, or to any part of that coast.

'Why Nice?' she asked.

'Because I've set up an interview with Giovanni Carlisle. His place is not far from Nice, just the other side of the Italian border. You can pick up a car at the airport and be there in less than an hour.'

Anny felt as if she were having a heart attack. There was a pain in her chest. She felt sick and giddy.

'It'll be the scoop of your career...the first time the King of Cyberspace has talked to a journalist. I hope you realise how lucky you are,' said Greg.

'Why send me? Why not someone who understands all that stuff?'

'Because it's the private man we're interested in, not the computer whiz. There'll be a file of clippings from the computer press waiting for you at the check-in. You can bone up on the technical background during the flight. This is your big break, Anny. You'll never get a better one. Go for it.' Greg rang off.

'What was all that about?' asked Jon, as she put the cellphone back in one pocket and the notepad in the other.

'An assignment to fly to Nice tomorrow...to interview Giovanni Carlisle.'

He looked relieved. 'That won't take long. You'll be back by tomorrow night. Until you said "Why Nice?" I thought it might be one of your editors sending you off to the back of beyond for a month. That would have been tough...just when I'm back for a spell.' As they began to walk on, he said, 'I thought Carlisle was famous for his hatred of the popular press and only ever talked to computer journalists on strictly technical matters.'

'Up to now, yes. But that makes him all the more desirable in the eyes of people like Greg. Most of the world's celebrities fall over themselves to get coverage. Those that don't—the ones who employ PR people to keep them *out* of the limelight—are the biggest quarries of all, from an editor's point of view.'

'I wonder why Carlisle has changed his mind?'

'I can't imagine,' said Anny. She thought, but didn't

say, And he may change it back double-quick when I turn up on his doorstep.

'I can give you a little bit of gen about him,' said Jon.

'You can?' Her eyebrows rose in surprise.

Jon had a degree in horticulture and now worked for Fauna and Flora International, an organisation dedicated to preserving natural species in their native habitats. He used a notebook computer and was sufficiently alert to what was going on in the world to have heard of Giovanni Carlisle, the genius behind Cyberscout. But she wouldn't have expected Carlisle to be more than a famous name to him.

'He lives at the Palazzo Orengo near Ventimiglia,' said Jon. 'From there to Cannes that whole coast is dotted with famous gardens planted when the Côte d'Azur was *the* smart place to go in the winter. Nobody went in summer. It was considered too hot. Orengo was one of the legendary gardens of the Edwardian era. Then its owner died and it began to decline...until Carlisle bought it. With the cost of labour sky-high now, only a billionaire could restore a place that size. But even the top brass at the Royal Society of Horticulture aren't allowed in to see what he's done to it. A guy I know who writes for their journal, *The Garden*, wanted to do a piece. He wrote to Carlisle, giving a string of influential references. He was turned down flat.'

'So why has he suddenly succumbed to Greg's blandishments?' Anny said, half to herself.

Jon could see she was totally preoccupied with the assignment. If she had had an inkling of what he was about to say before the telephone call, it had been driven from her mind. She was a dedicated journalist whose career, up to now, had come before everything. He accepted that. In some ways it was a bonus. It made her more understanding when his work took him away and kept her from being bored in his absence. Previous girl-friends had been less tolerant.

'I should think there's a lot of material about Orengo in its heyday in the RHS archives. I've got nothing to do tomorrow. If you like I'll go and dredge it out for you.'

'Sweet of you, Jon, but it could be a waste of time. Leave it till I get back. This whole thing could fizzle out if the so-called King of Cyberspace doesn't like my face.'

'Of course he'll like your face. It's a beautiful face,' he said fondly.

He was seeing her with the eyes of a man in love, but even people with clearer vision thought Anny Howard good-looking. In fact her eyes were her only truly beautiful feature; large grey eyes with dark-rimmed irises and long lashes. Men admired her slim figure and long legs. Women envied her style. Somewhere she had learnt the knack of wearing very simple clothes in a way that made them look better than expensive designer outfits on other women. But it was the warmth of her expression, the humorous curve of her lips, her attractive voice which drew people to her and made them confide in her.

Jon had wanted to marry her for months. Sensing that she was less sure of her feelings, he had been biding his time. In the event he had chosen his moment badly. That damned telephone call had come at the worst possible moment.

Now, with Giovanni Carlisle on her mind, it might be better to wait until she came back from France before broaching the subject again.

Late that night while, in London, Anny was checking that everything was in readiness for her early start to-morrow, in the balmier air of Monaco on the Riviera, a tall, dark-haired man in a dinner jacket was looking at the sculptured body of a naked girl with her forearms resting lightly on the shoulders of a naked man and her hands crossed behind his neck.

Giovanni Carlisle—known to his father's side of his family and to most of his intimates as Van—had seen the bronze before, but not by moonlight. It was by a sculptor called Kerkade who had called it *Invitation*. It reminded Carlisle of an incident in his own life.

The Principality of Monaco was not a place Carlisle liked. He never normally came here. But it would have been churlish to refuse the invitation to tonight's dinner party given by a woman who, like himself, was half-American. They had something else in common. They had both made serious mistakes in their personal lives, although his had happened in private, not in the glare of public attention which had surrounded her high-profile divorce.

Carlisle could never enjoy complete anonymity, but his life was as private as he could make it. Although rich and famous himself, he disliked the society of other people in that category. Most of the time he stayed inside the boundaries of his own smaller kingdom along the coast.

While Monaco's economy depended on the tourists who arrived by the coach-load to gawp at the soldiers from the Principality's minuscule army changing the guard outside the palace, Carlisle had no intention of allowing anyone to penetrate his seclusion except by invitation.

Thinking about the woman bidden to Orengo tomorrow, a cynical smile curled his well-cut mouth.

Was there a possibility that Anny Howard might put her pride before her career? Knowing her, he thought not. Much as she might dislike having to confront him, nothing would make her pass up an important scoop.

Teeth-gritted, she would come. But she wouldn't get what she wanted. He had made sure of that.

There was little traffic in the West End at ten minutes to seven next morning when Anny took a taxi from her flat to Liverpool Street Station where the seven-thirty Stansted Express would take her to the small airport thirty miles north of London.

The airport shuttle train took her to the final departure lounge where there were complimentary newspapers and a small quiet café serving Stansted's *habitués*. She needed a cup of coffee to pull her together after a disturbed night. Then she would look through the file on Giovanni Carlisle, the man whose brainchild, Cyberscout, had simplified public access to the vast resources of cyberspace and, in so doing, made him a fortune.

It was he, even more than Jon, who had kept her awake in the small hours and given her troubled dreams. She did not want to be here, on her way to Orengo. She had tried to forget the past and had thought she'd succeeded. Last night had proved that she hadn't.

Time, it was said, healed all wounds. What ailed her was like malaria in days gone by, a persistent infection which might recur for a lifetime. To know that in a few hours she would see Van again made her head ache, her body shiver.

She should have refused the assignment, made some excuse to get out of it. Why hadn't she?

Charlene Moore had been PA to Giovanni Carlisle for three years, since her predecessor, also American, had married a Frenchman from nearby Menton.

Charlene left the *palazzo* by the side door and walked down sloping paths and flights of steps to the swimming pool.

The extra-long pool had been sited where it could not
be seen from the house. It was filled with sea water
pumped up from the secluded bay at the bottom of the
huge garden. Every morning Mr Carlisle swam fifty
lengths before breakfast, although sometimes he didn't
have breakfast until ten or eleven, having worked most
of the night.

As Charlene had discovered in her first week at
Orengo, Mr Carlisle was a man who, as a poet had put
it, 'marched to a different drummer'. Other people's
ways of living and codes of behaviour meant little to
him. He could afford to do as he pleased, and did.

Although she lived on the premises, there were areas
of his life which even she didn't know about. It was
rumoured he had a beautiful mistress in Nice but, if so,
it was a discreet relationship. They were never seen together in public.

In some ways she felt sorry for him. He had a brilliant
mind, was phenomenally rich and also very good-
looking. But he would never know if a woman loved
him for himself or was only going through the motions
for what she could get out of him.

When she reached the clay-flagged terrace surrounding the pool, he was sitting at the far end, drinking coffee
and reading some papers.

Even at this early hour the sun was quite hot. The
breakfast table was shaded by a large square green
sunbrella. Her employer, wearing a white towelling robe
and navy cotton espadrilles, was sitting outside its
shadow, long suntanned legs stretched out and crossed
at the ankle. In addition to the thick black hair and olive
skin handed down from his mother's forebears, it
seemed he had also inherited a Latin liking for hot
weather. Even in the grilling heat of summer he never
looked hot or fatigued.

He saw her coming and stood up. He was always punctiliously polite, especially to his subordinates.

'Good morning, Charlene.' At the outset he had asked her permission to use her first name, but had never suggested she should be informal with him, even in private.

'Good morning, Mr Carlisle.'

He gestured for her to sit down in a canvas director's chair under the sunbrella. 'Did you enjoy your day off?'

'Yes, thank you. I went to Èze.' She was an amateur artist and spent her free time sketching the picturesque hill villages on both sides of the border.

As she took out her notebook in readiness for his instructions, he said, 'Later today we shall have a house guest...Anny Howard.'

He did not need to explain who Anny Howard was. One of Charlene's duties was to file all the British journalist's articles, sent in monthly batches by a London press clippings agency.

There had been several files full of clippings when Charlene started working here, and she had filled a couple more. Why Mr Carlisle was interested in Miss Howard was a mystery she had yet to fathom.

'Put her in the tower room, will you? Tonight have them use the round table, not the long one. I want Miss Howard opposite me.'

'That will make thirteen people. I know you are not superstitious, but it might worry some of your guests...and it would mean putting two women next to each other.'

'That would never do,' he said sardonically. 'In that case invite General Foster. He won't mind being asked at short notice.'

Charlene made a note to call the octogenarian Englishman who lived in a flat in Menton, a town once thronged by English winter sun-seekers. Even Queen Victoria had wintered there, renting one of the hotels.

'What time is Miss Howard arriving? You'll want Carlo to meet her, I presume?'

Her employer removed his sunglasses. Someone meeting him for the first time would expect his eyes to be brown to match the rest of his colouring. In fact they were blue, the vivid dark blue of a bed of echiums she had passed on her way to the pool.

'Her flight lands at four. There's no need to send the car for her. She's an experienced traveller and I'm sure the papers she writes for don't quibble about her expenses. We'll let her find her own way here.'

He spoke in his usual quiet voice, but it seemed to Charlene that his eyes had the steely gleam she had seen once or twice before when he was annoyed about something.

She had never incurred his displeasure and didn't expect to because she was very efficient. But she'd heard his wrath could be devastating. Other members of the household had told her, with graphic gestures, that when he was angry—*Dio mio!*—it was like a volcano.

Probably they were exaggerating. The Italian housekeeper and cleaners and the French chef were all inclined to make dramas out of minor incidents. They had more emotional temperaments than Americans and the British. But as Mr Carlisle was only half-American, perhaps he could be provoked into fiery eruptions.

Something was vexing him now. He was looking down towards the sea where the translucent blue-green water lapped against ochre rocks at either end of a scimitar-shaped pebble beach. The sight didn't seem to please him. His black brows were drawn together, his mouth set in a harsh line.

If Miss Howard's arrival was causing that grim expression, Charlene wondered why he was allowing her to come. Many well-known journalists had approached him for interviews, but all had been refused.

Why was he making an exception of Anny Howard?

Aboard Flight 910 to Nice, the cabin staff had taken their places for take-off.

Only five other people besides Anny were flying in the forward section. She put her tote on the aisle seat and the file on the seat next to hers. On her way to see anyone else, she would have been eager to start research-ing her subject. In this instance she wanted to postpone the study of Van's achievements since the last time she had seen him.

Instead she opened the in-flight magazine, but found herself reading paragraphs without taking in what they meant. She leaned back and closed her eyes, memories crowding her mind, the old pain lancing her heart.

That she was now five years older and far more sure of herself didn't make her confident that she would be able to handle him. She knew her defences would still be flimsy, her weapons feeble when matched with his formidable powers.

Van wasn't like Jon, kind and sensitive. In his field, Van was a genius, and like all such men he had a ruth-less streak. What he wanted he got. But he hadn't got her, or not on the terms he required.

That would have rankled for a long time. He might have forgotten her since then, but what if seeing her again rekindled his ire? Wasn't it better to avoid that possibility? When they landed at Nice, she could fly straight back to London. But if she did that what would it do to her prospects as a freelance journalist? Greg couldn't blame her for being thrown out by Van, but he would if she chickened out. She could say goodbye to any more assignments from him, and he might spread the word to other editors. Journalism was a competitive profession in which, so far, she had done well. That could change if she blotted her copybook with Greg.

Lunch was served. Anny had a good appetite and maintained her svelte shape with an energetic life rather than by counting calories. Today she did less than justice to an excellent meal.

With forty minutes to landing time, she broached the file, reading with practised swiftness clippings from the American and British computer press. Some of them carried the only photograph of Van ever released by his PR department. It showed him sitting in a swivel desk chair, a monitor screen behind him. His face was as she remembered it, not the way he would look now.

Replacing the clippings in the file, she took from her bag an envelope sealed five years ago and never opened until now. Her fingers weren't perfectly steady as she shook out the contents; several snapshots and various sentimental mementoes. It pained her to see them again. Greg, if he knew she had them, would badger her to let him publish them. Despite being taken by an amateur, they were valuable for the light they threw on the time before Van became famous.

Like Stansted, the airport at Nice was ultra-modern, built as close to the sea as it was possible to be. In the final minutes of the flight, Anny looked down at the familiar coastline, feeling a mixture of terror and joy.

Once these shimmering waters reflecting the blue of the sky had been her natural habitat. 'The nearest thing to a mermaid you'll ever see,' someone had said of her.

But that was long ago, when her skin had been almost always sticky from constant dunkings in the sea and her sun-streaked hair, when not hanging in dripping rats' tails, had been tucked up inside the straw hat she was made to wear out of the water.

Once through the airport formalities, which didn't take long these days, she looked around for a quiet corner from which to call Greg on her cellphone.

He was at his desk and took her call straight away. 'Hello, Anny. What's the problem?'

'No problems yet, but your briefing yesterday wasn't very informative. I'd like to know how you persuaded Carlisle to relax his embargo on journos?'

There was a pause before he answered. 'OK, I'll level with you. I didn't persuade him. He suggested it to me, but only on certain conditions.'

'Which were?'

'First, that I sent Anny Howard. It seems he's read some of your interviews and thought they were good.'

'What else?'

'He wanted a written assurance that he would be shown your copy before publication, with the right to make cuts…in fact to veto the whole thing if he didn't like it.'

'You didn't go along with that!' she expostulated.

'I didn't have any option. Anyway I'm sure he will like whatever you write. People always do. You're good at telling the truth in a way that doesn't upset them.'

'I wouldn't bank on that in this case.' Hot-tempered when she was younger, at twenty-five Anny had learnt not to fly off the handle even when raging inwardly.

'The fact that he specifically asked for you gives you a big edge,' said Greg.

That's all you know, she thought. Aloud, she said, 'Maybe…maybe not. I'll call you later.'

The girl at the car rental desk took her for a compatriot till Anny explained she was a foreigner. Her fluent French and Italian had been a help to her career, but she hadn't had to work at them like Jon with his Turkish. She had picked them up as a child, with some Spanish and Catalan learned in harbours and boatyards up and down the coast of Spain.

The fastest route from the airport to Orengo was by the coast road known as the Moyenne Corniche. But

Anny didn't want to join that shuttle of high-speed drivers and long-distance coaches. After Greg's revelation of who had really set up the interview, she needed time to re-think her plan of action.

All along the city's famous Promenade des Anglais people in warm-weather clothes were walking their dogs, jogging, or strolling with friends while teenagers on roller-blades glided past them. The palms, the tubs of geraniums, the awnings shading the windows of the hotels made her realise how much, subconsciously, she had missed this Mediterranean atmosphere.

Once this had been her world...

# CHAPTER TWO

SINCE the first time *Sea Dreams* dropped anchor in the quiet bay at the foot of the hill dominated by the dilapidated mansion called Palazzo Orengo, Anny had explored every corner of its neglected garden.

The last remaining gardener, an old Italian, had told Anny's uncle, the skipper of *Sea Dreams*, that the garden covered forty-five hectares. There had been a lot to explore. Of all its special places, her favourite was the belvedere with its views of the coasts of two countries, the Italian Riviera to the east and the French Riviera to the west.

The roof of the belvedere was supported by columns of carved rose-pink marble entwined by an old wisteria, veiling the building with its drooping clusters of pale purple flowers.

One hot afternoon, while Uncle Bart was napping in his cabin, Anny sat on the belvedere's balustrade, interviewing Doña Sofia, the Queen of Spain.

In her imagination, she had interviewed many of the world's leading women in preparation for the time when she herself would be one of the world's leading journalists. She had always known what she wanted to be. Journalism was in her blood. Her grandfather had edited a weekly newspaper, her father had been killed reporting a war in Africa and her uncle wrote for the yachting press.

There being no one to hear her except the small lizards which scuttled up and down the columns, she was asking her questions aloud.

19

'If you hadn't been born a princess, Your Majesty, what career would you have chosen?'

Before she could invent the Queen's reply, from behind her someone said, 'Who are you?'

The voice gave Anny such a start that she almost fell off the balustrade.

Standing in the entrance to the belvedere was a tall young man she had never set eyes on before. He was wearing a clean white T-shirt and dark blue jeans with brown deck shoes, the kind with a leather thong threaded round the sides. He had the same colouring as the youths in the nearby village, but their eyes were black and his were as blue as his jeans.

'I'm Anny Howard. Who are you?'

'Van Carlisle...hi...how're you doing?'

As she slid off the sun-warmed stone ledge, he came towards her.

As they shook hands, he said, 'Sorry I startled you. You must be the girl from the schooner down in the bay. Lucio told me about you.'

'Are you related to Lucio?'

'No, I'm related to the old lady who lives in the *palazzo*. She's my great-grandmother.'

'I've never seen her,' said Anny. 'Lucio calls her *la contessa*. Is she really a countess or is that just his name for her?'

'It's her official title, but she was born an American like me. The reason you've never seen her is because she's eighty-three years old and very frail. She stays in bed most of the time.'

'You don't sound like an American.'

'That's because when I was little my sister and I had an English nanny. My mother is Italian, my father's American and we lived in Rome until I was about your age. Tell me about you.'

'I'm an orphan,' said Anny. 'But I'm not unhappy like

the orphans in books. If I had parents like other people,
I'd have to live in a house. I'd much rather live on *Sea
Dreams* with Uncle Bart.' She looked at her watch. 'It's
almost time for his tea. Would you like to come down
and meet him? He's a very interesting man. He's sailed
all over the world. I've only sailed round the
Mediterranean a few times.'

'I've never had much to do with sailing people. Lucio
says this isn't the first time you've moored in the bay.'

'We come here every year. The berthing fees in the
marinas keep going up and we can't afford them,' Anny
confided. 'So we try to find moorings which are free.
There's a fresh-water tap and a lavatory in the beach
house which Lucio says the *contessa* wouldn't mind us
using. We help him in the garden for as long as we're
here.'

In fact it was only she who helped the aged gardener
in his vain attempts to keep Nature under control.

'How long do you stay?' Van asked.

'Two or three weeks, then we'll sail to Corsica. How
long are you here for?'

'The whole summer vacation. I'm at college in the
States. Where do you go to school?'

They had set out down the long path which, bisected
by many other paths, wound its way to the beach.

'I don't,' said Anny. 'Uncle Bart teaches me. We're
doing a special course to make sure I'll know enough to
pass some exams later on. At the moment I'm two years
ahead of my age group.'

Van was as tall as her uncle. Looking down at her,
he said, 'How old are you?'

'Nine and a quarter. How old are you?'

Her answer made him grin. 'Going on nineteen. What
happened to your parents?'

'My father was a television reporter. He and his
cameraman were ambushed by a group of rebels during

a war in Africa. That was before I was born. My mother died two years later. I don't remember her. There was no one else to look after me so Uncle Bart adopted me. The first thing he had to do was to drown-proof me so that if I fell overboard I wouldn't sink. Are you drown-proof?'

'I learnt to swim at school. I can't say I was crazy about it…or anything, except computers. Is your uncle teaching you computer skills?'

When Anny shook her head, Van said, 'You won't get far unless you're computer literate. Maybe I'll give you some lessons…get you started.'

'What is the child like?' asked the old lady propped up by pillows in the great carved and gilded bed. 'Is she pretty?'

'Not pretty, but very intelligent. More like thirteen than nine in her conversation. When they go to Corsica, maybe I'll sail over with them and come back on the ferry.'

'A splendid idea,' said the *contessa*, watching Van wolf down a large helping of pasta. 'It's not good to spend *all* your time riveted to your computer. I'm sure it's bad for you…hour after hour gazing at a screen.'

His mouth full, her great-grandson gave her a smile with his eyes. Although he was inches taller than her long-dead husband, and still far too thin for his height, there were moments when he reminded her of Giovanni, the irresistibly attractive Italian aristocrat who had come to New York looking for a rich bride to help him restore his ancestral home to its former glory.

Now, sixty-five years later, Orengo was again in decline. Very soon, like other once-great houses, it would be demolished and the site redeveloped as a hotel or blocks of holiday apartments. The thought of it tore at her heart but she could see no alternative.

Van was the only member of the family who ever came here and he was too young to rescue Orengo from the fate of all white elephants. Although several of his American forebears had made fortunes, he was unlikely ever to emulate them. He had a good brain but at present seemed unable to focus on anything but his computer.

Perhaps in twenty years' time he would be successful at something, but by then it would be too late.

On the morning of her sixteenth birthday, Anny was cooking breakfast in the galley when she heard someone hailing the schooner and went on deck to see Van standing on the beach with a knapsack slung on one shoulder.

Her heart leapt with pleasure. She hadn't known he was coming and having him to share her birthday celebrations was better than a stack of expensive presents.

'Watch the pan, will you, Bart?' she called to her uncle. 'I'm going to pick up Van.'

By the time the rubber dinghy nudged the shingle at the water's edge, Van had taken off his shoes in readiness to step aboard.

In the seven years since their first meeting he had changed as much as Anny had. The lanky youth, built like a half-starved dog, all ribs and prominent shoulder bones, had matured into a man with a lean but powerful physique.

Bart claimed some of the credit for this transformation. He had taught Van to crew for him and introduced him to the pleasures of snorkelling and wind-surfing. From being bookish and sedentary, he had changed, at least part of the time, to being an active outdoorsman.

'Hi! How's it going?' he greeted her.

'Fine. What a great surprise. When did you get here?'

'Too late last night to come down and say hello. Theodora says you were up at the house yesterday, writing letters for her.'

'Her hands are so twisted now it hurts her to hold a pen. But I thought she seemed less depressed. Did she know you were coming?'

He shook his head. 'I saw a special offer on trips to Paris. I have to be back there Thursday so I'll only be here two nights.'

'It's a long way to come for two nights.'

'I had a special reason. Bart...how are you?' Looking up from the dinghy as it came alongside, he gave his warm smile to her uncle who had come up on deck to greet him.

It wasn't till they were aboard and the two men had greeted each other that Van turned back to Anny. 'Happy birthday.' He bent his tall head to kiss her lightly on both cheeks.

Anny felt herself blushing. Kisses weren't part of her life. Bart was kind, but he wasn't demonstrative. Even when she was little he had never kissed her goodnight. Affectionate pats on the head or shoulder and, occasionally, a brief cuddle if she had hurt herself was his limit on physical expressions of the close bond between them.

Immediately after kissing her, Van started to delve in his knapsack, missing her reaction to the touch of his lips.

'A little something for the skipper...' he handed over a bottle in an airline bag '...and some bits and pieces for the first mate.'

The parcels he handed to her were all beautifully wrapped. Some of the ribbon adornments had become crushed in transit but were soon tweaked back into shape by Anny's appreciative fingers.

While Bart went below for a glass to sample his present, she began to unwrap hers, carefully peeling away the bits of sticky tape so as not to damage the lovely paper.

Members of Van's family whom she knew only by

name had sent a swimsuit, a calculator, a backpack-style bag, a pen as thick as a cigar, a belt with a silver buckle and a couple of cassettes for the head-set he had given her for her thirteenth birthday. All the presents had cards attached to them with messages like—*To Giovanni's mermaid with birthday wishes from Cousin Kate.*

The parcel tagged with his handwriting she kept till last. It looked and felt like a heavy book, perhaps an anthology of American poetry. He knew she loved poetry.

'You'll have to give me the addresses of all these kind people. I must write and thank them.'

'Postcards will do. You can buy some in Nice this afternoon.'

'Why are we going to Nice?'

'Wait and see.'

When Van looked at her with that glint of laughter in his eyes, it gave Anny a funny feeling in the pit of her stomach. She had felt it a few times before, like a butterfly fluttering inside her. Today it was stronger, more disturbing.

She read the card on his parcel. The message was short and factual. *To Anny from Giovanni.* With the date.

'Why not "from Van"?' she asked.

'Because that's my proper name. When I'm rich and famous I'll be Giovanni Carlisle to the world and Van to my family and friends. You won't use Anny for your byline, will you? I thought when you started your career you'd change to Annette Howard.'

'I like Anny better. It's what I've always been—' She broke off as, instead of the expected book jacket, she exposed a grey plastic box.

'What's that you've brought her?' asked Bart, reappearing with a bottle of whisky in one hand and two tumblers in the other. 'Will you join me?'

'Not right now, thanks. It's a laptop computer for

Anny to write her stuff on,' Van told him. 'That's a great
old typewriter you use, but it's a museum piece. This—'
he tapped the lid of the laptop '—isn't state-of-the-art,
but it's OK for entry level.'

Anny was overwhelmed. Because it was important to
Van, she had looked at computer equipment the last time
they were in a place with a shop which sold it. The
prices had seemed exorbitant.

Although Van's father had an important job in the
American foreign service and his mother's second husband had factories near Milan connected with the boom-
ing Italian fashion industry, Van did not seem to share
in his parents' prosperity. He had been expensively edu-
cated, but from things he'd let drop, it sounded as if what
he was paid for his job as a computer programmer didn't
leave him much spare cash after he had paid his over-
heads.

'Look, here's how you do it.' He showed her.

Watching the screen inside the lid come to life, she
said, 'It's wonderful, but you shouldn't have given me
such an expensive present.'

'I got it cheap from a guy who was upgrading. Later
I'll give you a tutorial. Right now, how about breakfast?'

'Oh, my goodness...the ham.' She handed the laptop
to him and hurried back to the galley.


Later they swam. Although here, in late April, the air
temperature was already that of midsummer in northern
Europe, when they dived from the deck, for the first few
moments under water the sea felt breathtakingly cold.
Bart never swam till June, sometimes not till July when
the water was as warm as consommé.

Their bodies adjusting rapidly, they struck out to a
group of rocks which offered places to sit.

'Why does your cousin Kate call me ''Giovanni's

mermaid''?' Anny asked, twisting her hair into a skein and squeezing the water from it.

'Once, when we were watching you swimming, Bart said you were the nearest thing to a mermaid I'd ever see. I must have told Kate that. Aah, this feels good.'

As he stretched out on the warm rock, his olive-skinned torso beaded with bright crystal drops, Anny felt another secret flutter. This time his stay was too short for him to tan deeply as he had when crewing.

'Will you come sailing this summer?'

'I don't think so.'

It hurt her that he didn't sound as disappointed as she felt. 'Why not?'

'Lack of time mainly. My collegiate life is over.'

After graduating summa cum laude—the equivalent of a first-class honours degree—he had gone on to do two years of post-graduate work.

'I'm part of the rat race now...as you will be pretty soon. Enjoy all this while you can. It won't last for ever.'

'I don't want to stay here for ever. It gets boring going round the same places year after year. I want to see Paris and London. But I worry about leaving Bart. I'm not sure he'll feed himself properly if I'm not around. He taught me to cook but he doesn't do much himself now.'

Van pulled his shoulders off the rock with the stomach muscles developed while mastering wind-surfing.

'You probably thought it wasn't such a good idea to bring him a bottle of booze. But Scotch is better for his liver than cheap plonk full of chemicals.'

Anny sighed. 'He drinks too much because he's lonely. An adopted daughter isn't the same as a wife. He was in love with someone a long time ago. But she wouldn't live on a boat and he knew the sea was in his blood. Imagine having to choose between the person you love and the only thing you want to do. It must have been awful...for both of them.'

'Forty years ago most women followed their men to wherever they had to go…darkest Africa…Patagonia…anywhere,' said Van. 'Sounds as if she wasn't really in love with him.'

'Or she may have known she couldn't cope. I've never been used to anything else so it doesn't seem strange to me. But it could be a difficult adjustment for someone brought up ashore.'

'An adjustment you'll have to make the other way round,' said Van. 'I wonder if you'll like big cities as much as you think.'

'Nice is a big city.'

'Nice has the sea on its doorstep. It's a village compared with Paris and London. Where I want to live is right here. But Orengo needs money spent on it…lots of money…the kind of money Theodora had when she came here.'

It was at his great-grandmother's wish that he used her first name.

'What happened to her money?' Until now Anny had never liked to enquire.

'The old boy blew most of it. They lived in tremendous style. There were fifteen gardeners and eighteen household staff. They entertained all the great names of their era, the Thirties.'

'Will you do that when you live here?' There was no doubt in Anny's mind that one day Van would be rich and famous.

'I shan't have thirty-three people on my payroll, that's for sure.' He looked at his waterproof watch. 'It's time we were getting back. Theodora wants to see you.'

He sprang up, holding out a hand to give Anny a pull-up. Their hands were only clasped for a few seconds, but the strength in his fingers, and the bulge of muscle in his upper arm as he lifted her to her feet with no effort on her part, reanimated the feelings she had had earlier.

Poised on the edge of the rocks three metres above the pellucid sea, they both inhaled a deep breath. In the first year or two of their friendship, this was a game Anny had always won. In those days she could hold her breath longer and swim further without tiring. Now the propulsion of Van's long, muscular thighs made him enter the water half a metre ahead of her, increasing his lead as they glided through the sunlit sea.

When Anny came up, gasping, he was still under the surface. She was swimming flat out when his dark head appeared, but he reached the schooner's ladder lengths ahead of her.

'It's time you had a handicap,' she said, as she stepped on deck with Van coming up behind her. 'You may not get as much practice, but you're so much taller and stronger.'

'OK, next time I'll give you a five-second start.' For a moment his blue eyes appraised her slender body in the new American swimsuit which had higher-cut legs and a more revealing top than her old suit.

Brief as it was, the look made her heart do a flip. Then Van turned away to pick up the towel he'd brought rolled round his brief black bathing slip.

Theodora di Bachelli was not in bed but sitting in a chair on the bedroom's awning-shaded balcony when Anny and Van entered her room.

'Many, many happy returns of the day, my dear child,' she said, holding out hands which now bore little resemblance to the bronze cast, made by an artist when she was twenty, on one of the tables in the shuttered salon.

'Thank you.' Anny bent to kiss the chamois-soft powdered cheeks.

'It's high time you had a dress,' said the *contessa*. 'As I can't come to help you choose it, Van will deputise for me. You can wear it tonight when you and your uncle dine here.'

'Uncle Bart hasn't any formal clothes,' said Anny. She had no intention of leaving him to eat alone.

'Neither has Van. Only you and I will dress up. I haven't dressed up for twenty years, but I shall tonight. A girl's sixteenth birthday is a special occasion. Imagine, I was only two years older than you when I married. My husband was twenty-five, the same age as his great-grandson.' After glancing at Van, she went on, 'But in those days well-bred young men in their twenties spent their time sowing their wild oats. Do you understand that expression?'

'It means having love affairs, doesn't it?' Anny replied.

'Love affairs of a nature which might be condoned by their fathers but were not approved of by their mothers—if they knew about them,' said the *contessa*. 'Young men would also get drunk and, if they were very wild, smoke opium. As the French say, the more things change, the more they remain the same. The only difference between my time and your time is that now many good girls do what once only bad girls did and drugs are on sale everywhere.'

Van said dryly, 'We're not all doing drugs, Theodora.'

'I'm sure you have too much intelligence to jeopardise your future. *Your* only excess, that I know of, is straining your eyes, doing whatever it is that you do on that machine you installed in the tower room.'

She turned back to Anny. 'You, my dear, have had the good luck not to be exposed to bad influences. I hope you will always stay as unspoiled and lovely as you are today. If I were your fairy godmother, I would use my magic to make sure that when you are a little older you will fall in love and stay in love for the rest of your life.

It doesn't happen very often, but it did to me and I hope it will to you.'

'Thank you, Contessa...and thank you for the dress.'

It was the prospect of going shopping with Van, rather than the dress itself, that made Anny's eyes sparkle.

'Why do the rest of your family never come here?' she asked, on the train which ran from a station near the *palazzo* to Nice, sometimes snaking into tunnels where the mountains came down to the sea and re-emerging into the sunlight above bays where the clear water showed where the sea-bed was sandy and where it was covered with dark green weed.

'They couldn't very well come here and not stay at Orengo. By their standards it's falling to bits,' Van told her. 'Americans are accustomed to a higher level of comfort than any other nation. They had central heating and showers decades before Europeans. They don't like insects and draughts and damp-smelling closets. Orengo is stuck in a time warp. It was the height of luxury in its day, but that was a long time ago.'

'You like it. You're American.'

'Not really. Do you know the expression "a citizen of the world"?'

Anny shook her head. Bart had bought her a set of encyclopaedia, but it was out of date by twenty years. As they only ever saw newspapers and magazines which other people had discarded, sometimes there were embarrassing gaps in her general knowledge.

'It means someone who feels they belong to the human race rather than to any one country,' he explained. 'I go a step further. I feel I belong to cyberspace. Right now it's like the old Wild West...unexplored territory. But one day...'

As he explained his vision, Anny listened intently, as she did to everything Van said. But a lot of it was be-

yond her comprehension. She wondered if there was a
book on the subject she could study before his next visit.

'If this were New York we could go to Bloomie's,
but here I wouldn't know which is the best store,' said
Van, on arrival at Nice.

'That's no problem,' said Anny. 'Let's have a drink
in one of the cafés and when I see someone going past
who looks the way I'd like to look, I'll ask her where
she shops.'

The suggestion seemed to amuse him. 'Do you really
have the nerve to do that?'

'Why not? It's common sense. Who minds being told
you like the way they look? Anyway I can't afford to
be shy if I'm going to be a journalist. I'll have to persuade other people not to be shy with me.'

They chose a café in one of the pedestrianised shopping streets near the western end of the spacious Place
Massena with its public gardens and fountains.

Presently, while she sipped a soft drink and Van had
a beer, she saw a couple of girls a little older than herself
whose style she wanted to emulate. Flattered by her ex-
planation, they were only too ready to list their favourite
shops.

'There…you see? One easy movement,' said Anny,
returning to their table outside Le Paradis.

'You should have offered to buy them a drink,' said
Van. 'The one in blue had excellent legs.'

The remark sapped all Anny's pleasure in the success
of her strategy. She felt furious with him.

'If you want to pick up girls, you'll have to do it
yourself.'

Van laughed, showing his white teeth and giving her
another of those strange little internal tremors. She didn't
like the way his blue eyes were following another girl
passing by, one closer to his age than the other two.

She knew that in a white shirt and much laundered

jeans she was no match for the local girls, all of whom seemed to have that elusive quality called chic. Their figures weren't better than hers, and not all were prettier. But they all had something she lacked and was eager to acquire, even though she couldn't pin it down.

Van finished his beer. 'When you're ready, we'd better get started.'

While he paid the waiter, Anny finished her *jus d'orange*.

The girls to whom she had spoken had explained the location of the shops they recommended. Anny had half expected that Van would remain outside, perhaps suggest meeting her later. Her uncle had given her the impression that, except in places like a ship's chandler, the male sex was not at ease in shops.

Van, it seemed, was an exception. He not only came inside the shop but suggested they should both trawl the racks and pick out what caught their eye.

'What size are you?'

Anny consulted an assistant who looked her over and decided she was a 36. Having heard them speaking English, she added that this was the Continental equivalent of an American 8 or a British 10.

After looking at several price tags, Anny went back to Van. 'These are all very expensive. I don't think the *contessa* realises how much dresses cost now. If she's short of money...'

'She's not *that* short of money,' he said. 'She's a very old lady. She may not be around next year. Let her enjoy being generous.'

Of the three dresses she took to the fitting room, two were possibles and one impossible; but she couldn't resist trying it on and then showing it to Van, hoping it might make him see her from a new perspective.

It was made of a clingy red fabric with a halter-necked

glittery bodice cut in a way that made a bra unnecessary for anyone with firm breasts.

Barefoot, because her sandals spoiled the effect, she walked out of the fitting room, wondering how Van would react. While she was fastening the zip, she had heard the salesgirl practising her English on him.

Seeing Anny got up like a swinger gave Van a curious jolt. He had noticed that morning that she had a very good figure, but now, with every curve emphasised by a low *décolletage* and hip-hugging skirt, it was hard to believe that here, metamorphosed into a sexy young woman, was the androgynous child he had found acting out a daydream in the belvedere.

In a few years' time she was going to be drop-dead gorgeous. Right now she was barely sixteen and although she already had a shape that would knock guys' eyes out if they saw her in that red outfit, to anyone with a grain of intelligence it was obvious that she didn't have the experience to handle the reactions the dress invited.

'Uh-uh,' he said, shaking his head. 'That little number would give Theodora heart failure. Try these two I picked out for you.'

Anny looked doubtfully at his choices, neither of which appealed to her. 'I'll show you my other two first.'

'OK.' He resumed his conversation with the salesgirl.

Anny had thought he was only interested in computers. But this afternoon he was behaving like what Bart called a skirt-chaser. She didn't like it. She wanted him to concentrate on her.

When she appeared in the next dress, a more sedate style splashed with pale pink roses on a turquoise background, Van said, 'That's pretty, but the shoulders don't fit and you'd need to replace that tacky plastic belt.'

He was equally critical of her third choice, giving Anny the feeling she must have disastrous taste.

Trying on one of the dresses he thought suitable, she had to admit it looked much better on her than it had on the hanger. It was cream cotton, overchecked with white, with cream lace cuffs on the short sleeves and a triangle of lace sewn into the low V-neck. The waist was tight, the full hem almost down to her ankles. Reluctantly, she acknowledged that it was more becoming than any of the previous three.

'Theodora will like that,' said Van, when he saw it. 'How do you feel about it?'

'It's all right.' She wasn't going to enthuse after he'd been so stuffy about the red dress.

On the morning of her seventeenth birthday, Anny took the dress from the hanging locker in her cabin where it had stayed, unworn, since the year before.

Tonight there would be no celebration. The *contessa* was in a private clinic, having tests. Bart had had to go to England for the funeral of his eldest sister. Anny hadn't gone with him because they were short of money. Even one air fare had left their resources at a worryingly low ebb.

She was keeping her fingers crossed that an article she had sent to a French magazine would be accepted. They had taken a previous piece and paid her a useful fee. But she couldn't count on it happening a second time.

She took the dress on deck to give it its fortnightly airing. When, if ever, would she wear it again? she wondered forlornly.

She hadn't seen Van since last spring because, although he had been to Orengo in the interim, she and Bart had been away. At least when they were at sea Bart drank less, but to Anny it had been deeply frustrating to be somewhere else while Van was at the *palazzo*.

On one of his visits, he had left a portable printer for her. By then she had mastered the word processor and,

with the addition of the printer, was able to produce
professional-looking typescripts.

Bart wouldn't hear of her leaving home before she
was eighteen. Meanwhile she was working hard to build
up a portfolio of freelance published work to show to
prospective employers when she applied for staff jobs.

Since the *contessa*'s admission to the clinic, Anny had
been hoping that Van might come over to see her. Her
relations in America knew where she was because she
herself had called her younger sister in Boston to tell
her about the tests. Anny had dialled the number for her
on an old-fashioned daffodil telephone with the numbers
in holes in a metal disc the *contessa* found awkward to
use now that her knuckles were swollen.

Now, looking up towards the house with its flaking
pink-washed walls and peeling dark green shutters, her
attention was caught by a splash of coral-red on the long
staircase which was the garden's main axis. Lucio didn't
have a shirt that colour and anyway he wouldn't be coming down the stairs two at a time. Only one person ran
down them at that breakneck speed.

Anny leapt to her feet. He *had* come. In a few minutes
he would be on the beach, waving to her.

Her life, which for twelve long months had been like
a ship in the doldrums, the zone of calm weather along
the equator where, in the days of sail, vessels had been
becalmed, was suddenly back in motion.

# CHAPTER THREE

'YOU'VE cut off your hair!' he exclaimed, as she cut the dinghy's motor to glide the final few metres.

'Do you like it?' she asked, stepping out of the dinghy.

Van bent down to beach it for her. 'I don't know...takes getting used to. You look different...not a mermaid any more.'

'I couldn't stay a mermaid for ever. It's great to see you.' She stepped forward, offering her cheek.

For a few seconds, his hands rested on her shoulders and she felt the masculine texture of his cheek against hers, once, twice and a third time. 'Good to see you too, Anny.'

'Have you seen the *contessa* yet?'

'I stopped off at the clinic on my way through Nice. She's enjoying being the centre of attention and all the comings and goings. It must be hellishly boring, cooped up in her bedroom here. Bart's gone to England, I hear. How long will he be gone?'

'Only a week.'

'Why didn't he take you with him to meet your other relations?'

'Apart from the sister who has died, he doesn't get on with the rest of them.'

'I don't think he should have left you here on your own,' he said, frowning.

'Why not? I'm a big girl now.'

'That's why. These days there are people around who, if they knew you were alone, might make trouble. You do bolt the main hatch at night?'

She nodded. 'We do that even when Bart's at home. It isn't necessary here, but sometimes we berth in places where things get stolen even with the owners on board. Usually on boats where there's been a party and everyone ended up stoned from drink or dope.'

He said, 'Why not sleep at the house until he comes back? I would come and sleep in Bart's cabin but he might not like that. Here—' he indicated the *palazzo* '—there's Elena to make it respectable.'

The thought of Van sleeping on board *Sea Dreams* had been in Anny's mind many times. She had often fantasised about sailing somewhere, alone with him.

'Why wouldn't it be respectable without Elena?' She knew why, but wanted to hear him explain it. 'I've read that in New York and London young people often share houses. No one thinks anything of it.'

'That's different. There's usually a group of them sharing to pay a high rent, and the girls aren't as young as you are. I haven't said happy birthday yet. I left your presents on the terrace.'

'It's nice of you to remember.' She sent him cards on his birthday, but up to now had never had enough money to mail a gift to the States.

'Have you worn your dress since I last saw you?'

Anny shook her head.

'You can wear it tonight. We'll go to the clinic together, spend a while with Theodora and then have a seafood supper in the old part of town. How does that sound?'

'It sounds wonderful.'

The *contessa* received them in a bed jacket of peach satin edged with swan's-down over a nightgown trimmed with hand-made lace. Her white hair, as fine as spun sugar, was brushed into an aureole like the pale glow surrounding saints' heads in mediaeval paintings.

'Except when they stick needles in me, I am enjoying this experience,' she said cheerfully. 'Here is a little gift for your birthday, Anny. It's time you began to wear make-up, but only a soupçon. Try not to overdo it. You have a lovely skin and beautiful eyes. A little colour on your lips and a touch of scent here and there is all that you need at present.'

The parcel she took from the night table and handed to Anny contained a lipstick and a small bottle of perfume.

'The scent is Fragonard's *Rêve de Grasse* which, as you know, means ''Dream of Grasse''. One of the nurses lives at Grasse and I asked her to go to the Fragonard factory for me. I used to go there every year to buy scents and soaps and cosmetics. This scent is also sold by one of the most famous Paris couturiers, but he has re-named it Poison. I hope it will suit you. To smell exquisite, a woman must find a scent that combines with her natural aroma. Open the bottle and try it. How do you like Anny's new hairstyle, Giovanni?'

'I liked it long,' he answered. 'Shall I deal with that?' He stretched out his hand for the scent bottle which had a sealed glass stopper.

Anny handed it over and Van produced a pocket knife. When he had removed the seal, he put his finger on the stopper, turned the bottle upside down and then, standing it on the tray-table at the foot of the bed, used one hand to lift Anny's hair away from her ears and the other to touch the skin behind her lobes with the wet stopper.

'And on her wrists…where the pulse beats,' said the *contessa*.

Already quickened by the brush of Van's fingers against her ears and neck, Anny's pulse accelerated like a car competing in the Monte Carlo Grand Prix when he turned her hands palm upwards to do as the old lady bade him.

'By the time you've tried out the lipstick, we shall know if you smell like a dream...or poisonous,' he teased her.

The lipstick was the soft pinky-beige of weathered Roman-tiled roofs. It toned with the soft golden colour of Anny's skin and, combined with the natural rosiness of her lips, emphasised the shape of her mouth and made her feel much more sophisticated.

They spent an hour at the clinic and then, suddenly, the *contessa*'s animation waned and in a matter of moments she had fallen into a doze. As her naps usually lasted some time, her visitors quietly withdrew. At the desk at the end of the corridor, Van left a message with a nurse that he would come back in the morning.

The clinic overlooked the Promenade des Anglais and had once been a hotel as grand as the Negresco.

'I wonder what it costs to eat there?' said Anny, as they walked past that imposing edifice, built in the style of a wedding cake with a pink fish-scaled dome from the top of which the French flag fluttered in the pleasant sea breeze of a fine spring evening.

'A lot,' said Van, 'but you wouldn't like it in there.'

'Why not?'

He shrugged. 'It's not our sort of place.'

She was pleased by the implication that they were two of a kind with the same tastes and preferences. But the journalist in her made her ask, 'How do you know? Have you been there?'

'No, but you only have to look at that outfit the doorman's wearing to know what it's like inside. I prefer the simple fish restaurants near the flower market. Which reminds me...' Van put his hand on her shoulder, making her come to a standstill.

Stooping, he sniffed, 'Mm...that scent suits you.'

As they moved on, Anny noticed that Frenchwomen of all ages from teenage girls to women with matronly figures looked with interest at the man strolling beside her. Most young Frenchmen were taller than their fathers and grandfathers, but few were as tall as Van or held themselves with his air of assurance.

She basked in the pleasure of knowing that this evening she looked like other girls of seventeen and was out for the evening with a man who might be considered a bit too old for her now, but wouldn't always be. Each year the age gap between them would become less important. She just had to pray that he wouldn't fall in love with anyone else before she was ready for love. Seventeen was too young. She knew that. But eighteen was officially grown-up and nineteen was old enough for anything…even marriage.

The thought that in two years from now they might be walking hand in hand, and before the evening was over Van might have proposed, led her thoughts into the future.

Noticing her pensive expression, Van said, '*Rêve* can also mean daydream, can't it?'

'Yes…or illusion. Why?'

'A scent meaning daydream has to be right for you. You spend most of your time in a daydream.'

'Not most of it…only some of it. Doesn't everyone?'

'At seventeen, yes, I guess so. By the way I've asked another friend to join us. She lives in Nice. I met her last time I was here. Her name's Francine.'

Anny felt her happiness evaporate as if it had been a balloon and he had deliberately punctured it.

'Where did you meet her?'

'I needed to buy some disks. Her father owns a computer store. Francine was filling in for her mother who works there. She's at college, studying computer graphics for a career in magazines. She could be a useful contact for you.'

As soon as they met, Anny knew that Francine felt the same way about her as she did about the glamorous French girl. It amazed her that Van didn't sense the antipathy between them, but he seemed unaware of it, his mind focused on the menu and wine list with the same serious attention the locals gave to their food.

Because the evening was so mild they were able to sit outside, under the restaurant's awning. The two girls sat opposite each other with Van next to Francine. This made Anny feel even more of an interloper.

The meal was delicious but she would have enjoyed it far more had she and Van been *à deux*. First they had a thick fish chowder with large chunks of crusty bread. The waiter left the silver tureen and its ladle on the table. Francine had one helping, Anny two and Van three.

Then came a silver dish like a cakestand supporting a mound of crushed ice on which was arranged a variety of sea food.

Van and Francine were drinking wine, but for Anny, to her chagrin, he had ordered *jus de pomme*.

At least Francine had the grace to wish her a happy birthday. Perhaps if they had met in different circumstances they might have found things in common apart from the company of a man neither wished to share with another female.

It was clear that from Francine's viewpoint the evening ended too early. She lived on the outskirts of Nice. Van put her into a taxi and discreetly paid the fare. Then he and Anny went home by train.

Van was not at Orengo for her eighteenth birthday, but she wasn't too disappointed because he had already arranged to join them on board *Sea Dreams* when they sailed from the Riviera to Port Mahon, the capital of Minorca, the most northerly of Spain's Balearic Islands.

Anny was overjoyed that he would be spending his vacation on the schooner. She hoped it would be a repetition of the good times they'd had among the Greek islands when he was at college and she was a carefree child.

Now the time was near when she would have to leave Bart and go ashore to earn her living, she was less carefree. The *contessa*'s health was another worry.

'It's time I was gone,' she would say, several times a week. Then, reaching for Anny's hand, forgetting she had expressed the same thought many times before, she would say, 'I have had the best of my life. It's such a bore, being old. How I envy you, dearest child...all the excitements ahead of you...falling in love...getting married...having babies.'

Anny did not say so but, in her opinion, while love and marriage and children were still extremely important, for her own generation of women another ingredient was needed to make up a happy life. Without a successful career, and the independence and fulfilment resulting from it, how could a woman feel she had justified her existence?

She wished she had someone with whom to discuss her career plans. Bart refused to accept that she was old enough to leave home. He regarded big cities as sinks of iniquity and thought eighteen was too young for her to be exposed to the hazards of life in Paris.

Anny hoped that while Van was with them he would back her desire for independence. She knew Bart's opposition was partly because he would be lonely without her and loneliness would make him drink more.

But common sense told her she shouldn't put off her departure because of Bart's dependence on her and the bottle. He had been both father and mother to her and she loved him and worried about him. But he was not yet an old man. The only way she could care for him when he *was* old was by establishing herself in a well-paid profession.

A fortnight before Van's arrival, she received payment for French syndication rights to an article. The money paid for various urgent necessities with enough over for Anny to feel justified in buying herself a denim skirt and a Sunday-best T-shirt with printed cotton appliqués on the front and back.

Two days before Van was due to arrive, he telephoned the *palazzo* and left a message with Elena that he would be bringing a girlfriend.

Anny was furious. 'What cheek! He should have asked your permission, not taken it for granted.'

'He knows we have room for her,' said Bart.

'If she's anything like Francine, she'll be nothing but a nuisance,' said Anny. 'I don't know what he saw in her. I thought she was a pain.'

'Maybe this one will be better. Maybe this time it's serious,' said her uncle. 'How is he to know the sort of girl he prefers if he doesn't try a selection? All the time he was at college, he concentrated on his studies. For several years after that he was obsessed with computers. They're still his primary interest. But he's a fine, virile young chap. He's not going to stay a bachelor for the rest of his life.'

His words plunged her into gloom. If it turned out that Van *was* in love with this girl he was bringing, how could she bear to watch them being all lovey-dovey?

Instead of counting the days to his arrival, she began to dread the confirmation that Van's heart was given to someone else.

Right at the back of her mind where she didn't have to acknowledge it, even to herself, she had believed Van was hers...had always been hers. They might even have been together in some previous existence, although she wasn't sure she believed in that possibility.

What she was certain about was that she and Van belonged together and it had been destiny, not chance, which had brought him to Orengo at a time when *Sea Dreams* was moored in the bay below the *palazzo*.

When Van and his friend arrived, Anny was in the *contessa*'s bedroom, reading aloud to her. Voices and footsteps on the stairs made her pause. Moments later there was a familiar knock at the door and Van walked in accompanied by a red-haired girl whom Anny would have liked to dislike on sight but had to admit was strikingly attractive.

As he crossed the room to embrace his great-grandmother, Van gave Anny a smile. After greeting the old lady with his usual warmth, he introduced his companion.

'Theodora, this is Maddy Forrester. She's the great-granddaughter of a friend of yours, Virginia Forrester…Virginia Ferguson as she was when you knew her.'

The discovery that Van and the redhead had links going back to the time when the *contessa* was young made Anny's spirits sink even lower. But when it was her turn to be introduced, she forced herself to behave as if she was delighted to meet Maddy.

Two days later, most of which Van had spent in the old lady's company, leaving Maddy to get to know the Howards, *Sea Dreams* left her anchorage on a south-west course for the Balearics.

'Thanks for looking after Maddy for me,' said Van, following Anny below decks while Bart was letting the American girl take the helm for a short time. 'I wanted to spend as much time as possible with Theodora. She's aged a lot, hasn't she?'

Anny nodded. 'I don't think she's going to be here very much longer,' she said sadly.

'When I saw how things stood I wanted to cancel the trip and stay with her,' said Van. 'Maddy wouldn't have minded. But Theodora wouldn't hear of it. She became quite distressed.'

Anny knew, but perhaps he might not, that Theodora's husband had proposed to her when they had both been guests on a large and extremely luxurious American yacht. Perhaps she hoped history would repeat itself and by the time they returned Van and Maddy would have sealed their relationship on board the schooner.

'When you said you were bringing a friend, we assumed she was coming with you from America,' she said, starting preparations for lunch. 'Then Maddy explained she lives in Paris. I'm hoping she'll convince Bart that if I get a job there I won't be risking my neck every time I go out of the door.'

Van stationed himself where he wouldn't be in her way. In the confined space between decks he seemed even larger than usual.

'Maddy's been there a couple of years. I expect she's told you she works for the Paris bureau of CNN. Her brother and I were at college together so we go back a long way. But there was a break of a few years before we ran into each other while she was back in New York. D'you like her?'

'Who wouldn't?' said Anny, rinsing lettuce.

'How's the writing going? What have you sold since I last saw you?'

She told him, adding, 'Van, would you look at my CV…tell me how to improve it?'

'Maddy's your best advisor. We'll both look at it for you.'

'Thanks.'

But Anny didn't want their combined opinion. She wanted to recapture, if only briefly, the close companionship of previous voyages.

Expecting to see them exchanging ardent looks and surreptitious caresses, she was relieved that they were very discreet. At night she lay in her cabin, listening for sounds that would indicate Van was leaving his cabin to go to Maddy's. The thought of them making love made her bury her face in her pillow.

She could come to terms with his previous girlfriends. At his age it was inevitable he would have had other girls. But Maddy was different. She came from his own milieu, had known him for years and would be approved of by his family.

More than that, she was nice. In every way, from her age to her background, she was perfect for him.

But did she love him as much as Anny did? Would she go through fire and water for him?

The Mediterranean could be treacherous. Halfway to Port Mahon, with nowhere to run for shelter, *Sea Dreams* was hit by a squall. It didn't bother Bart or Anny, and Van had proved himself a good sailor during a spell of rough weather on their way to the Greek islands.

Maddy quickly discovered that she was not. At the first sign of bad weather, Bart gave her an anti-seasickness pill, but it wasn't effective. As soon as the schooner started rolling, she began to be violently ill. She was also terrified, convinced they were all going to drown.

To leave her alone would have been cruel. Anny stayed with her, trying to convince her that *Sea Dreams* had weathered much worse 'blows' than this and was virtually unsinkable when handled by a skipper of Bart's experience and with a crew as competent as Van.

Eventually the squall abated and Maddy, exhausted, slept. Glad to get out of the cabin, Anny put on her foul-weather gear and her life-jacket and went on deck, inhaling deep breaths of fresh salt air.

Van was with Bart at the helm.

'How is Maddy?' he asked. Like Bart, he didn't look tired but rather exhilarated.

'Sleeping. She's had a bad time. I don't think she'll want to see you until she's recovered a bit.'

'As soon as we've berthed she'll be fine,' said Bart. 'Being seasick is like having a baby, so they say. Bad at the time, but soon forgotten when it's over.' He smiled at Anny. 'You gave your mother a spot of bother, but the first time I saw you I could tell she thought you were worth it. When we sail into Port Mahon, Maddy'll forget her troubles. It's a magnificent harbour. We always enjoy ourselves there.'

They spent two days in Minorca and it seemed that Maddy had recovered and was enjoying herself. But the night before they were due to sail round the coast to Ciudadela, a picturesque town at the other end of the island, she announced that she couldn't face it.

They were in one of the harbour's restaurants, waiting for their meal to be served, when Maddy dropped this bombshell.

'I'm sorry. I shouldn't have come. I had no idea I was such a terrible sailor...or that it would be so rough. I couldn't go through that again. I just couldn't.'

'It's most unlikely we'll run into more bad weather,' Bart assured her.

'I'm not prepared to risk it. I can fly back to Paris from here.'

Taking it for granted that Van would go with her,

Anny felt like bursting into tears. It was all going from bad to worse. She had an ominous feeling she might never see him again.

Then, to her surprise, Maddy added, 'Don't feel you have to leave with me, Van. Flying doesn't scare me and I've never been airsick. But, unlike the three of you, I'm a rotten sailor. To be truthful, I wasn't too happy when the water was calm.'

Expecting Van to insist on going with her, Anny was even more astonished when he said calmly, 'I'm sorry it's turned out like this.'

'I don't understand it,' said Anny, when Van had gone to see Maddy off from the airport. 'I thought they were in love.'

'What gave you that idea?'

'Why else would he bring her?'

'Ask him. I can't tell you.' Bart was in one of his irritable moods. 'She hadn't much pluck. The chances are it'll be as calm as a millpond from now on.'

Perhaps, thought Anny, Maddy's defection had reminded him of the girl who had blighted his life by refusing to sail the world with him.

When Van returned, Bart was having a siesta. Anny had decided she couldn't go on wondering about the exact nature of the others' relationship.

'I thought Maddy was your girlfriend.'

'I thought I was doing her a favour, bringing her here,' Van said dryly. 'We were both wrong.' He sat down in a deck chair and stretched his long legs. 'Maddy has a broken heart. I expect it will mend in time but right now she badly needs something to take her mind off her trouble. I thought a sea trip would be perfect. Who would have guessed she'd be one of those people who throw up if there's a slight swell running?'

'Who broke her heart?' asked Anny.

'Some bastard who forgot to mention he was married.'
He gave her a thoughtful look. 'I don't know what made
you think she was my girl. A schooner the size of *Sea
Dreams* isn't the ideal venue for people who want to be
alone together. The bunks are only marginally wider
than coffins, apart from Bart's which is shaped like a
wedge of Brie.' Amusement tugged at his mouth. 'Also
there are "noises off" which aren't too romantic…like
someone pumping the loo on the other side of the bulk-
head.'

Anny, her world set to rights, burst out laughing. 'I
hadn't thought of that. I suppose, if you live in a house,
life on a boat does take some getting used to.'

'And vice versa, as you'll find when you get a job.
You said you wanted me to look over your CV.'

From then on it was like old times. Bart woke up in
a better mood and they went by dinghy to a secluded
bay where the two younger people swam and he fished
from the rocks.

On their last night at Port Mahon, again they ate out.
Anny wore her new skirt and T-shirt and she and Van
joined the *paseo* of evening strollers. Bart preferred to
sit outside a favourite bar where they would join him
later.

'I wonder if journalism is the right career for you,'
Van said, after suggesting a further improvement to her
CV.

'What a strange thing to say. It's the *only* career for
me.'

'It's changed since your grandfather's time, even since
your father's time,' said Van. 'Unless you see television,
you have no idea what a swarm of blowflies the press
has become, and not only the tabloid press. The broad-
sheets have ditched most of their ethics as well. Anyone
in the news can't set foot outside their front door without
being mobbed by photographers and reporters. I can't

see you pushing and shoving to thrust your recorder under the nose of someone whose life is in ruins.'

'I don't want to be a news reporter. I want to be a feature writer.'

'Most of them do a hatchet job. The bigger the byline, the more snide the comments,' said Van. 'I think you'd be a lot happier working for, say, an academic publisher. You're not tough enough to be a journalist.'

'How can you say that? You don't know what I'm capable of.'

'I have a pretty good idea. I've known you a long time.'

'You still think of me as a child,' she said angrily. 'I'm not. I'm grown-up now…a woman.'

'Only just,' Van said, smiling. 'You're tough in situations you're used to, like that squall the other night. But I'm not sure you'd do so well in Maddy's environment…the rat race.'

'I'll survive,' Anny said confidently. Then, anxiously, 'If you start on this tack with Bart, I'll never forgive you. I need you on my side, not against me.'

'I am on your side, but I know more about city life and the pressures and stresses than you do.'

'You know a lot about cyberspace. It doesn't make you an expert on other people's career choices. The *contessa* thinks you should have gone into banking. From what I gather, your entire family thinks you're wasting your potential.'

Van shrugged. 'That's because they haven't grasped that we're on the brink of another "giant leap for mankind". Anyway it's not my future we're discussing, it's yours.'

'My future's been settled for years. You've seen my portfolio. If I didn't have what it takes, those editors wouldn't have bought the pieces I offered them.'

'There are thousands of freelances around, not many

of them making enough to live on. The competition for
staff jobs is a lot tougher.'

'I know that. I'm not an idiot,' she said indignantly.
'I don't need all this wet-blanket stuff. I get enough from
Bart. What I need from you is support.'

By this time they were almost back to the café where
Bart was watching the promenade of local people and
tourists.

When Van ordered fruit juice for her, red wine for
Bart and a beer for himself, Anny said to the waiter in
Spanish. 'Not fruit juice…a glass of white wine, please.'

Her uncle's attention was elsewhere but Van lifted an
eyebrow, his blue eyes amused by her assertiveness.

'When did you start drinking vino?'

'Ages ago.' She had sometimes had sips of Bart's
wine, but the first full glass she had drunk had been
champagne at the *palazzo* at Christmas. The *contessa*
had a glass of champagne every evening. She called it
her pick-me-up. Anny found it rather dry and hoped the
café house wine would be a sweet one.

As they waited for the waiter to return, she was con-
scious of Van's rangy body at ease in the chair next to
hers. Bart's belt was hidden by the overhang of his
paunch which each year grew a little fuller. Van's mid-
riff was flat and, as she had seen while they were swimming, there was much more muscle than flesh cladding
his long, lithe frame. He fitted into the Mediterranean
scene as if he belonged here, as in a way he did. Even
his vivid eyes did not mark him out as a tourist because
quite a few Menorquins had eyes which were not dark
brown.

Anny's sun-bleached hair springing from fair roots
marked her out as a foreigner who might be looking for
holiday romance.

In the restaurant where they ate, a young man at the
next table, part of a large family party, kept looking at

Anny, attempting to catch her eye. At first she ignored him. But after a while, piqued by Van giving his whole attention to Bart, she responded to the Spaniard's glances in the way she had seen other girls look at admirers.

Annoyingly, Van seemed not to notice this silent flirtation going on under his nose.

But later it turned out he had. When they returned to the schooner, after Bart had gone to the heads, Van said, 'Sending come-on signals to boys you don't know isn't a good idea, Anny. Don't say "I don't know what you mean". You do, and you did, and if we weren't leaving tomorrow you could find yourself being targeted not just by him but by the guys he hangs out with. These young studs compete with each other to score with available girls.'

Anny felt herself flush a deep red. Unable to defend her behaviour, she resorted to attacking his. 'I suppose you speak from experience, having "scored" with Francine and others.'

But it gave her no satisfaction to see, by the hardening of his mouth, that her riposte had hit home.

Bart reappeared. 'Make a pot of tea, will you, Anny? The pork has given me heartburn. If I don't take a tablet I'll be awake half the night.'

An hour later, he was snoring. But it wasn't that which kept Anny wakeful. It was the row with Van which she knew had been her own fault. How could she have been so stupid as to open a rift between them just when things had begun to go right?

In the morning there was nothing in Van's manner to alert Bart to the fact that his crew had had a disagreement. The moment her uncle was out of earshot for a few minutes, Anny intended to make peace.

But a suitable opportunity didn't arise and presently the two men went ashore, Bart to have his hair cut and

Van to go to a hotel where he could use his modem and check his electronic mailbox.

Left on her own, Anny did some cleaning. So far Bart's weakness for the bottle had not caused his standards to decline. Old as she was, *Sea Dreams* still looked immaculate and, whenever she was berthed in a harbour, always attracted a lot of admirers, especially among people who preferred the graceful shape of an old-fashioned sailing vessel to that of a modern motor yacht.

Presently Anny heard someone calling *'Señorita!'*. She put her head out of the main hatch to see if it was her attention they were trying to attract. To her dismay, the young man from the restaurant was standing on the quay, smiling at her.

Out of politeness, she stepped on deck and said good morning in Spanish. That was her second mistake.

# CHAPTER FOUR

WHEN they were short of money, Bart looked for the cheapest berth, however inconvenient. This time, because he had recently received the half-yearly income on his small amount of capital and also because they had had two visitors on board, her uncle had chosen a quayside berth.

As soon as she said good morning the young Spaniard came on board. 'Ah, you speak Spanish,' he said, smiling. 'That's good because I have not much English.'

'How did you know where to find me?' Anny asked.

'When you left the restaurant with your father and the other man, I followed you. I wanted to talk to you. I can see you are busy now—' he looked at the polishing cloth she was holding '—but will you come for a walk with me this evening?'

'We're leaving here today.'

'What a shame. Will you come here again?'

'I don't know. Not for a long time.'

'Too bad. My name's Salvador. What's yours?'

'Anny.' She couldn't help feeling flattered that he'd made some excuse to leave his family in order to follow her. Although he could not compare with Van, by ordinary standards he was a good-looking youth and from a respectable background. His family had been well-dressed and well-behaved. She couldn't believe he was the kind of youth who belonged to a gang of yahoos.

'This is a beautiful boat,' he said, looking up to the top of the mainmast. 'I've always wanted to learn to sail. Your father doesn't need an extra hand, does he?'

Anny shook her head. There seemed no point in explaining that Bart wasn't her father.

'Do you have a job?' she asked. Perhaps he was still at college.

'My father's a builder. I work in the office. One day I'll take over the firm. But it's a dull life,' he said, with a grimace.

After some more conversation, he asked her to show him round. By now convinced he was harmless and feeling sorry for anyone chained to a desk when they longed for a more adventurous life, Anny took him below to see the main cabin and the galley.

He seemed so interested in everything—the stove mounted on gimbals, the stowage areas and especially the navigation area with its chart table, VHF radio and some electronic aids Bart had installed—that it came as a surprise when he put an arm round her and kissed her.

'You're very pretty, Anny. I wish you were staying longer.'

'No, Salvador…please don't…'

Blushing, she tried to push him away. His kiss had been gentle and not unpleasant, but she didn't want him to repeat it.

Salvador put both arms round her and kissed her again, this time less gently. Anny began to worry in case things got out of control. Seconds later they were; Salvador fired up like an outboard motor, his excitement embarrassingly obvious even before she felt his tongue in her mouth.

Revolted, she used all her strength to shove him away from her. At the same moment they both heard footsteps on deck.

'*Fuera!*' Anny said fiercely. It was the Spanish equivalent of 'Get lost!'

She didn't need to repeat it. Salvador shot through the hatch. Then she heard Van say, 'What the hell…?' followed by a series of thuds, a yelp and a gabble of agitated Spanish.

'Anny…are you there?' Van shouted.

Guessing he thought he had intercepted a sneak-thief, she hurried on deck to find he had grabbed Salvador and was holding him by the scruff of his shirt.

Looking scared, Salvador gabbled in Spanish, 'I didn't mean any harm. It was only a kiss, for God's sake.'

'What the hell is going on? Did you ask him on board?' Van demanded.

No wonder Salvador was frightened. Anny had never seen Van in this mood. His face was a mask of anger, his eyes like lasers. The plastic bags he'd been carrying when he stepped aboard had been dropped, their contents scattered.

'Please…let him go,' she begged. 'He hasn't done anything wrong.' She knew that what Salvador had done had been in part her own fault for agreeing to show him below.

'So why was he bolting?' Van said harshly.

She could see there was nothing for it but to tell him the truth. 'He…kissed me. I told him to beat it. That's what he was doing.'

'In that case I won't delay him.' Van grabbed the Spanish youth's shoulders, swung him round to face the stern and knee-kicked him in the backside, sending him flying quay-wards, arms flailing to stop himself falling.

He managed to keep his balance and stumble up the gangplank. Once on the quay he found the courage to turn round and shout some angry remarks at the American. But when Van took a single stride forward, Salvador decided not to risk being grabbed a second time. Flushed with rage and humiliation, he ran.

Van turned and looked at Anny.

She said hurriedly, 'I know…you don't have to tell

me it was stupid of me to show him round. But he seemed so nice…so interested…'

'"Stupid" isn't the word for it. A girl alone on a boat who lets a stranger go below has to be out of her head,' he told her, his tone like a whiplash.

'I know and I'm sorry I did.' Her lower lip trembled.

'Is that all he did? Kiss you?'

'Yes, but it wasn't nice. He…it was disgusting!' Feeling that if she didn't wash her mouth out she might be sick, she hurried below.

She had gargled with some of Bart's mouthwash and was brushing her teeth over the washroom basin when Van's reflection appeared in the mirror. During the day, except when the heads were in use, all the doors between decks were left open, clipped to the bulkheads.

'Are you OK?' he asked, in his normal tone.

Her mouth full of toothpaste, she nodded.

'I'll make some coffee,' he said. 'We'll have it on deck.'

The awning rigged to make shade had been taken down, but at this time of year it wasn't intolerably hot as it would be in July and August.

With the coffee, Van brought a bar of chocolate. 'My cousin Kate has a saying "When men are unbearable, take a double dose of choc".'

Anny managed a shaky laugh. She liked the sound of his cousin and hoped one day they might meet. Snapping the bar in two, she handed half back to him.

'Let's both have a dose. Girls are unbearable sometimes…like me last night. I didn't mean to snap at you. I knew what you said made sense.'

'What happened just now…was it happenstance?' Van asked. 'Were you on deck and he came by?'

'He followed us back last night. I think he *is* interested in boats. Kissing me was…an impulse.'

'An impulse which a lot of young guys are going to

feel when they're with you. Maybe no one's explained to you that males between sixteen and twenty have a problem controlling themselves if girls lead them on, or *seem* to be leading them on,' Van added, as she opened her mouth to protest. 'You're growing very pretty, Anny, and you're a natural blonde which is always an extra switch in countries where most girls have dark hair.'

'Is it? I'd rather have dark hair, or lovely red hair like Maddy's.'

Van gave a theatrical groan. 'Why are women never satisfied with the way they are? Even the ones who look great are always worrying about the size of their breasts or their backsides or whether their nose needs re-shaping. There must be millions of bottle-blondes who would give a year's salary to have hair your colour, especially when it's combined with dark eyebrows and eyelashes. Most girls as fair-skinned as you have to have them tinted.'

That he had noticed these details sent her spirits soaring. He must have studied her more closely than she had realised.

'Did you read that or did one of your girlfriends tell you?'

'I must have read it somewhere. You're the only blonde in my life,' he said teasingly.

'Does that mean you personally don't find blondes attractive?'

'I don't classify women that way,' he said, suddenly serious. 'A thing you should know about guys is that up to a certain age, or stage of development, they're likely to be attracted to any passable female. Basically all they want is a girl they can take to bed. Then, if they have any brains, they begin to see women as people they can talk to and have a good time with out of the sack as well as in it.'

He reached out to take her half of the chocolate wrapper, scrunch both halves together and put them in his pocket until he was near a waste bin.

'In a few years from now I'll be looking for someone to marry and it won't be her hair or her legs that will draw me to her,' he went on. 'It will be her character. If you're going to spend your life with someone, you need to enjoy the same things, laugh at the same jokes, have the same goals on your life list.'

'What are the goals on your list?'

'The big one is making my fortune. My best chance of doing that is to dream up a great piece of software millions of people will buy.'

'I don't want to make a fortune. Only to earn enough money so that Bart can always keep *Sea Dreams*, even if she's permanently berthed. I don't want him, when he's old, to be stuck in a room with a lot of other old men and a TV switched on all day. I know how much he'd hate that.'

'If my plans work out, I'd like to help,' said Van. 'Bart means a lot to me too. Including Theodora, the four of us are like family. We aren't always together, but there's a close link between us.'

Did he mean he thought of her as an unofficial sister? Anny wondered, downcast. It was not how she wanted him to see her.

Perhaps her dismay was visible. He said kindly, 'Are you still upset by that young dolt making a hash of your first kiss?'

'What makes you think it was my first kiss?'

'The way you've been raised plus your reaction,' he said dryly. 'Not going to school, you haven't had a chance to mix with boys the way most girls do. Was I wrong?'

Anny shook her head. 'If that's what I've missed, I'm glad,' she said vehemently.

There was a hint of a smile at the corners of Van's

mouth as he said, 'Don't decide you don't like it on the basis of one bad experience. There are kisses and kisses. It sounds as if that young jerk went too far too fast. What he should have done—'

Because of the limited deck space, their chairs were not far apart. He leaned towards her, taking her chin in his hand and tilting her face.

'Is this,' he concluded, before brushing her lips with a kiss which only lasted a moment but was the most thrilling sensation she had ever experienced.

For a few seconds afterwards he kept his hand under her chin and there was an expression in his eyes she had never seen before and hoped might mean that his feelings were not, after all, as fraternal as she had feared.

Swept by an overwhelming impulse, she said, 'Van, will you make love to me?'

The silence that followed her question seemed to last for ages. She couldn't tell what he was thinking and she couldn't think what had impelled her to ignore conventional constraints and say what was in her mind.

Yet, strangely, she didn't feel embarrassed. It was what she wanted. Why not say it? If she couldn't speak freely to Van, whom she loved, who could she open her heart to?

He let his hand fall and sat back, his expression withdrawn and unreadable.

'No way,' was his slightly curt answer.

'Why not?'

'Because you're too young and Bart trusts me not to get out of line.'

'I'm not a child any more. I can decide for myself now.'

'No, you're not a child, but you're not quite a woman yet.'

'I shan't be a woman till someone makes love to me. I'd like it to be you.'

'I'm flattered you feel that way, Anny. But as you've had an unusual life so far, why not keep it that way? Why not be really unusual and save making love for later? There's no law that you have to do it before you get out of your teens: if not there's something wrong with you.'

'I know that. But I can't help being curious. Surely everyone is? I don't want my first experience to be a huge disappointment like the way Salvador kissed me. When you kissed me, it was…lovely. I'd like you to teach me everything. Then I won't be tempted to try it with someone who might be hopeless at it.'

Van clapped his hands on his head and screwed up his eyes. It was a gesture and grimace she had seen once or twice before when he couldn't believe what he was hearing.

A few seconds later, he resumed his previous posture. Speaking slowly and quietly, as he did when explaining something about computers to her, he said, 'When you fall in love with someone, and he loves you, he won't be hopeless at it, Anny. It'll be great for both of you. The magic ingredient is love. Without that, sex is about as satisfying as a fast-food beefburger. Believe me: I've been there, done that and don't recommend it, especially not for a girl.'

'Why is it different for a girl? That's a sexist attitude.'

'It's horse sense. However equal we are, we're always going to be different. Men can have sex and walk away and forget it. Maybe a few women can, but mostly they can't. They get hurt or they feel remorse. It does bad things to their psyche, leaves them all mixed up. Drink your coffee before it goes cold.'

She did as he told her, the euphoria induced by his kiss beginning to die down, making her regret her openness. Had it spoiled their friendship? Would he think less of her now?

'Have you ever been in love, Van?' she asked.

'If I had, I'd be married. They say children of divorced parents have a hard time keeping their own relationships on track. Maybe…maybe not. There've been a lot of divorces in my family. I don't plan to add to the total. When I marry it will be for keeps.'

'How can you be sure?'

'Marriage isn't that difficult. People go into it for the wrong reasons. My father married my mother because she was beautiful. She married him to get away from her family.'

'You told me your great-grandfather married the *contessa* for her money. Yet they were happy.'

'The way she tells it, yes. I suspect she closed her eyes to a lot of extra-marital affairs a modern wife wouldn't tolerate. Theodora has a Continental attitude to marriage. Over here they think marriage and the family is too important to allow it to fall apart because of temporary difficulties. The Americans and the British think everyone is entitled to be happy all the time, which is crazy. Anyway these are issues you don't have to think about for several years yet. We'll discuss them again when you're older and have your career organised.'

'But I'm interested now,' she persisted. 'There's no one but you I can discuss these things with. The *contessa* doesn't understand the way people live today. Bart's not comfortable talking about emotional things. I've sometimes thought that might be one of the reasons why the girl he loved wouldn't marry him. Apart from not wanting to live on a boat, she might have found him too reticent.'

'Here he comes,' said Van, looking along the quay.

'Right, let's be on our way,' Bart said, as he came aboard.

The routine for leaving a berth differed from harbour to harbour. Anny knew them all, but waited for his instructions. While Van was on board she had much less to do than when there were just the two of them.

As they sailed out of Port Mahon's vast harbour where once a great fleet of British sailing ships had sheltered and where, according to an unreliable legend, Admiral Lord Nelson had occupied an elegant house on the far side from the town, she wondered if this might be the last time they would come here as a threesome.

Although Van had said he felt linked to them, when the *contessa* died, which could happen any time, inevitably the link would be weakened. Once Anny was working, her holidays might not coincide with his.

The pattern of their lives was changing. Part of her was eager for the new experiences and wider horizons the changes would bring. Part of her longed for everything to stay the same.

As *Sea Dreams* left the shelter of the harbour for open water where a strong breeze was blowing and the surface of the sea was choppier, it seemed to symbolise the impending transition in her life.

But even if she never came to Port Mahon again, she would always remember it as the place where Van had kissed her.

The turn-around point of the voyage was Jávea, a town on the east coast of Spain. They had been to Jávea many times, but never with Van on board, and she was eager to show it to him; the fisherman's church like an upturned boat, Polly's Bookshop, the shingly cove called the priest's beach at the foot of towering red cliffs and the walk along the top of the massive sea wall protecting the harbour.

It was while they were berthed there that Anny saw a side of Van which was new to her.

The day they arrived he bought a copy of an English-language newspaper published for the large community of American, British and other expatriates in the area. Reading it, he discovered the town had a club for English-speaking computer buffs. When he rang up the secretary to ask if he might attend a meeting, their conversation led to his being invited to stand in for a speaker who had been taken ill.

Anny went with him to the bar where the meetings were held. As there had been no time for him to prepare a presentation, she was nervous for him. While the chairman of the club was introducing him, her stage-fright was almost as intense as if she were speaking herself.

But when Van rose to his feet, relaxed and smiling, his vivid eyes scanning the faces of the much older men who were his audience—there were far fewer women present—she sensed it was going to be all right.

When, forty minutes later, he sat down, she was awe-struck not only by his vision of the future but by the fluency with which he expressed it. Resounding applause was followed by many questions, but after the chairman had thanked him and others had made it clear they would like to buy him drinks and continue talking to him, Van excused himself.

'Were you bored rigid?' he asked her, as they started walking back to the harbour.

'You can't be serious. I was riveted. They all were. I'm sure now you will make your fortune. I had no idea you could be so...dynamic.'

He laughed. 'People with obsessions can be world-class bores, so I try to keep quiet about mine except when I know I'm with people who share it.'

'I don't think anyone there had a fraction of your expertise.'

'They haven't grown up with computers the way we

have. But they're proving it's not a technology only the young can understand.'

Nothing untoward happened on the homeward run, but when they got back to Orengo, Lucio, who had seen them approaching, was waiting on the beach to tell them the *contessa* had died in her sleep the night before.

Most of her friends having died before her, she had left instructions for a small private funeral. She was buried in the family vault with her husband and his forebears in the presence of her great-grandson, the Howards and her surviving retainers. By the time they heard of her death, it was too late for any of her Italian and American relations to attend, if indeed they would have made the effort except in the expectation of receiving a legacy.

The *contessa*'s will was short and straightforward. Apart from bequests to her servants, everything she possessed had been left to Van. But the generous legacies to Elena and Lucio had exhausted her financial resources. Van had become the owner of a once-magnificent house and vast garden with no means to maintain them.

Word of her death spread quickly. With unseemly speed Van was besieged by offers from developers. He could have become rich overnight for the land surrounding the *palazzo* was the finest site on the Riviera di Ponente.

Bart thought him mad to refuse the offers.

'What's the point of hanging onto the old place? You're never going to live here,' he said.

'I shall live here and so will my children and their children,' Van said, with conviction. 'Anyway property values are subject to booms and busts like everything else, but they always go up in the long term. If the garden becomes a jungle, it doesn't matter. One day I shall have the money to put it back in order.'

Bart thought he was talking nonsense. At increasingly infrequent intervals Bart was writing his yachting articles on an antiquated typewriter, pecking at the keys with two fingers. He refused to learn how to use Anny's laptop and would never adapt to the computer age or grasp the exciting concepts Van had outlined in his talk to the club in Jávea.

Before the *palazzo* could be closed up, decisions had to be made about all its contents. Most of the furniture, including many valuable antiques, was already under dust covers. Van felt the risk of theft was outweighed by the high cost of storage in a repository. The sale of one or two of the least desirable pieces would finance the installation of electronic eyes monitored by a local security firm catering to the many rich people with valuable possessions in the area. These devices were thought to be more of a deterrent to thieves than complicated locks and iron grilles.

He asked Anny to help him sort out the *contessa*'s personal possessions. While he worked his way through the old lady's cluttered writing desk, every pigeon hole and drawer stuffed with papers, Anny sorted out a chest of drawers, finding exquisite underwear which had never been worn and boxes bearing the names of shops in London, Paris and Venice, containing fans, gloves, embroidered handkerchiefs and scarves.

In her will the *contessa* had expressed the wish that if there were things in her wardrobe Anny liked and could make use of, she was to keep them as an inadequate reward for her many kindnesses to an old lady.

One morning, before she had started to tackle the wardrobes, all of them, like the drawers, lined with sandalwood so that it had never been necessary to put old-fashioned moth balls, with their pervasive reek,

among the *contessa*'s clothes, Anny arrived at the house
to find that Van had already made a selection.

'You're going to need a lot of clothes when you start
work. Last night I picked out some I think will suit you.
They may need a few alternations, but the quality of the
materials and the finish is better than anything in the
shops today. Even some of the styles are back in fashion,' he told her.

She wondered how he knew that, but was more curious to see his idea of what would suit her.

'Try this on for size. It looks as if it would fit you.'
Van lifted down a hanger he had hooked over the top
of one of the wardrobe's doors. On it was a close-fitting
short-waisted pale grey jacket made of a fine wool cloth
whose name Anny didn't know.

She buttoned it over her T-shirt. It might have been
made for her.

'You could wear it with this black skirt,' said Van,
taking down another hanger.

She unzipped her jeans, stepped out of them and took
the hanger from him. The skirt was lined with black silk.
It had a caressing softness against her bare legs as she
fastened the waistband.

When she looked up, Van said, 'Don't strip off as
casually as that in front of other guys, will you? They
might get the wrong idea.'

She felt herself starting to blush under his quizzical
scrutiny. Her briefs being no more revealing than the
bottom half of her swimsuit, she had acted without thinking.

'I wasn't showing anything you haven't seen a million
times when we're swimming.'

'But this isn't the beach,' he said dryly. 'Try the rest
on. I'll leave you to it.' He walked out of the room.

Bart came ashore to join them for lunch on the terrace.

'It will seem strange, coming here and finding the old

place closed up,' he said, with a sigh.

'I'll be back as often as I can,' said Van. 'I'm fixing up the rooms in the tower. Elena will have a key. She'll come in to open the windows so the place doesn't get too musty.'

He turned to Anny. 'I've E-mailed some people for advice on what to do about Theodora's clothes. It seems we have two options. All the top auction houses have offices in Monte Carlo. We can ask them for expert valuations. Or we can contact museums which hold big collections of period costumes. What do you think?'

'Would the museums pay for the clothes, or would they expect to be given them?'

'They have funds to buy for their collections, but whether they'd offer as much as auction buyers might...who can say?'

That afternoon Anny opened a long cotton bag and found inside it a dress of such irresistible glamour that she couldn't resist trying it on although only to see what it did for her. By this time she had discovered that, at an earlier stage of her life, the *contessa* must have had a lady's-maid who had put little numbered tags on all the hangers with the same number on boxes containing shoes and other accessories.

The dress was made of sea-green dévoré velvet. Anny wouldn't have recognised it if she hadn't browsed through a copy of *Vogue* in a paper shop while they were in Spain. The magazine had included a feature on the velvet and the costly process which removed the pile from the silk backing, leaving only the design in velvet. On the *contessa*'s dress the design was of long swirling leaves, their fluid shapes defined by crystal beads, tiny silver spangles and rhinestones. The dress itself was of the utmost simplicity, sleeveless with a low neckline and an even lower back.

Wearing only her briefs, Anny slipped it over her head and let it slither into place, clinging to her body from breast to knee before flaring to a hem which lay in a pool round her feet until she put on the shoes made from the same material with high heels of silver kid. There was also a matching envelope-shaped evening bag lined with silver kid.

Walking carefully on the elegant heels, she went in search of Van, hoping the sophisticated dress would make him see her from a new perspective.

She found him in one of the corridors leading from the main staircase to rooms which for several decades had only had their shutters opened two or three times a year.

'I've found the key to this cupboard. It's full of old photograph albums,' he said, without looking up from the album he was studying.

It surprised her a little that although he knew it wasn't Elena—she had painful feet and shuffled around in slippers—he didn't register the difference between Anny's leather-soled Greek sandals and the click of high heels on marble.

'Perhaps, somewhere, there's a picture of the *contessa* in this dress.' She struck a pose: one knee forward, a hand on her hip, the other holding aloft the evening purse. 'How do I look?'

His expression abstracted, he glanced at her. Then, as he took in the dress, the album was thrust aside and he rose to his feet.

'You look fantastic. Where did you find that outfit?'

'Hidden away in a bag. Isn't it fabulous? It must have been made for a very special occasion. I wish I knew what.' She turned to display the back, watching him over her shoulder.

For a minute, before he masked it, the look on his

face was what she had hoped to see. But as she revolved to face him the revealing glimpse disappeared.

'Perhaps we can find that out. The costume experts should be able to pinpoint the year it was made. That will give you a lead.'

'Somewhere around there are records of all the parties the *contessa* gave and went to,' said Anny. 'Hostesses kept ''accounts'' of what ''chops'' they owed and to whom. She told me about it one day when she was reminiscing.'

'Anyway that's one dress that won't be going to auction or into a museum,' said Van. 'You must keep it for when you're reporting a gala occasion.'

'No, no, I couldn't. That's not why I put it on…as a hint that I'd like to keep it. I only wanted to…' She realised she couldn't explain her real motive.

'I know you didn't, but you must. It makes you look like a mermaid coming out of the sea. I expect Theodora had forgotten she had it. If she had remembered, she would have wanted you to have it.' He snapped his fingers, struck by something he had forgotten. 'There's a letter for you.'

From the back pocket of his jeans he produced a long white envelope.

Anny took it, recognising it as one of the self-addressed, stamped envelopes she had sent with her job applications. It was postmarked Paris. Before she opened it, she had a premonition it was going to change her life.

# CHAPTER FIVE

ANNY'S first job wasn't the one she wanted, but it was a start.

She was taken on as a junior assistant in the editorial department of a news magazine. This meant that she was a gofer who did whatever menial tasks were required of her, including going out to buy sandwiches for editors lunching at their desks.

She learnt a lot by listening and watching and the personnel director who hired her had said that if she proved useful, after a year, if a junior vacancy occurred on the editorial staff, she would be considered for it.

Anny saw Van more often than she had expected. He had contacts in Paris. He seemed to have contacts everywhere, people he'd got to know in news-groups on the Internet.

On one of his visits he brought her a modem for her laptop computer so that they could E-mail each other instead of communicating by fax or telephone. She was happy that he wanted to keep in close touch with her, although the tone of his letters was too 'elder brother' for her liking.

She also saw a lot of Maddy, who had organised her accommodation. It was a room in an apartment with two American girls, both of them personal assistants to executives on the Paris staff of American corporations. They had a lot of friends and gave frequent parties at which Anny found herself blandished by a cosmopolitan selection of attractive men.

Not that they were attractive to her. Only one man was that. But she accepted some of their invitations, solely in order to describe where they took her to Van. One of her dates was a young American architect, in Paris on a scholarship.

One night, without advance warning, Van turned up at the flat. The others were out and Anny had been working on an article she hoped to sell to a travel magazine. She had already had a snack supper and Van had eaten on the plane. While she was making coffee, he said, 'You seem to be seeing a lot of this architect.'

'Tom is showing me the city…places I wouldn't find by myself.'

'I expect you would if you bought yourself a good guide book.'

'Plodding round with a guide book wouldn't be as much fun. We have a good time together.'

'Has he made a pass at you yet?'

She opened a carton of milk. 'I don't know how you define a pass,' she said coolly.

'Has he tried to get you into bed?'

'That's classified information. I'm sure you wouldn't like it if your girlfriends disclosed intimate details of your behaviour to all and sundry.'

Van's jawline hardened as if he were clenching his teeth with exasperation.

'I'm not ''all and sundry''. In Bart's absence, I'm the nearest you have to a family.'

'Bart wouldn't cross-examine me about my friends.'

'Maybe you don't tell him how often you're seeing this guy? Are your letters to Bart the same as your E-mails to me?'

One of the advantages of using a word processor was that the same basic letter could be adapted to suit different recipients. Anny did copy the news she had written to Van in her regular bulletins to her uncle. But then she deleted all the bits she had put in hoping that, if they didn't succeed in making Van jealous, they would at least remind him that she was someone other men took an interest in.

'Not entirely. You and Bart are interested in different things.'

'We're both concerned that you don't have the same family back-up as other girls. I know more about the hazards of big city life for a girl your age than he does. In Bart's day the rules were different. Dates didn't end in bed. All the pressure came from parents, not from peer groups.'

The coffee tray being ready, he stepped forward to carry it through to the living room for her.

'I've never had a peer group, or not until recently. If I listened to Fran and Julie, I'd never go to bed with anyone. Hearing them talk about their experiences isn't encouraging. Most of the men they've slept with have been pathetic in bed.'

This was an exaggeration. When they were her age, both her flatmates had had some disappointing experiences which they'd described to Anny with wry amusement, in the hope of discouraging her from similar acts of misjudgement. Now, in their middle twenties, both were involved in serious relationships with men they wanted to marry but who, having been married before and divorced, were reluctant to risk a second commitment.

Their advice to Anny was to concentrate on her career and stay clear of emotional entanglements until she was securely established. For her, this was easy, but she hadn't revealed to them that her heart was already engaged. Her feelings about Van went too deep to be discussable with anyone.

While he was pouring the coffee, Van picked up her last remark.

'Perhaps they had unreasonable expectations,' he said

dryly. 'Sex is like ballroom dancing. Both partners need to know the steps to put on a dazzling performance.'

'I'm sure Fran and Julie do. It was the men who didn't. According to them, great lovers are in short supply.'

She thought he might be annoyed by this aspersion, but he only shrugged. 'They may be right. If I were you, I should assume they are and stay out of close relationships. In a few years' time you'll find yourself liking someone for all the other reasons that form rock-solid bonding.'

'Which are...?'

'You know them as well as I do. A similar background...common interests...the same sense of humour...shared aspirations.'

'I have those with Tom,' said Anny. 'Not the similar background, but all the others.'

'How old is he?'

'Twenty-four.'

'He's too young to be serious about any girl.'

'Oh, come off it: lots of people are married with children at his age.'

'And lots of people have split by the time they're twenty-five or twenty-six. You want to stay married, don't you?'

'Of course. So does everyone. But sometimes it doesn't work out.'

'It stands a better chance of working out if people get their own lives organised before they take on the responsibility of making someone else happy.'

'I expect so, but falling in love doesn't always happen at the most suitable moment. I can't see myself saying "no, thanks" to the love of my life because he happens along a year or two early,' Anny said, copying her tone from the most flippant of the magazine's staff reporters.

'If you're the great love of *his* life, he won't go away.'

Van sounded irritated. 'Falling in love is an illusion anyway. I'm not saying it doesn't happen, but it doesn't last. I sometimes run into guys I knew at college who can't remember the names of girls they were crazy about ten years ago.'

Anny heaved a long-suffering sigh. 'Van, you're lecturing. I don't need all these instructions about how to run my life. I'm a big girl now. I support myself…just! I pay tax. I have a career plan. I'm not about to foul that up by getting myself pregnant or doing anything stupid. Why can't we talk about something really constructive—' she gave him a mischievous smile '—like computers?'

An unwilling grin relaxed the strong, raw-boned face which seemed to become more attractive each time she saw him. After his last visit, she had overheard Fran and Julie talking about him, agreeing that if they hadn't been committed already they would have been madly attracted.

'He's one of those men,' Fran had said, 'who behaves like a perfect gentleman, but you feel that somewhere inside there's a gene handed down from someone lawless and wild. Perhaps it won't ever surface, but you have the feeling it might.'

They were in the kitchen when this conversation took place. Anny, in the living room, hadn't seen Fran's expression, but she had heard Julie's reply.

'I know what you mean. Yes, if someone drove him too far, I think Van could become *very* uncivilised. I'm glad Don's not like that. A man who looks dangerous can be very exciting, but what would he be like to live with? I'd rather have someone tamer and less unpredictable.'

Recalling that conversation, while sitting opposite its subject, Anny knew what they meant. With her knowledge of his background, it was easy to visualise someone closely resembling the tall, rangy man on the sofa as the leader of bandits in the mountains of Italy, or an outlaw riding alone through the American West in the days when only rough, tough men could survive there.

While these thoughts were in her mind, Van rose and went to the black nylon-canvas case he had left on a chair by the door. Unclipping one of the side pockets, he took out some floppy disks.

'These are some programs which might be useful to you. Fetch your laptop, will you? I'll install them for you.'

Anny felt her pulses quicken. Sitting close to Van while he did what he called 'housekeeping' on her computer was one of her life's secret pleasures.

She would have preferred to join him on the sofa, but when she came back from her room, Van had moved to the dining table. As he took the laptop from her, their fingers touched. He would never guess that slight contact had far more effect on her senses than other men's kisses.

'What's your password?' he asked.

'I haven't changed it. The chances of anyone guessing it's *Sea Dreams* are pretty remote, don't you think?'

'I guess so.' His long square-tipped fingers were light and expert on the laptop's keyboard. Unlike Bart, he was not what was jokingly known as a biblical typist, meaning someone who used two fingers while searching the keyboard on the 'seek and ye shall find' principle. Van had learnt touch-typing from a program he had later passed on to Anny.

The laptop's small screen gave her a good excuse to shift her chair as close to his as it would go and then to lean even closer. Being near to him made it hard to concentrate on what he was saying, but she knew that she must or he might ask her a question she wouldn't be able to answer.

Having installed the new programs, Van gave short demonstrations of how they could be useful to her. He was an excellent teacher, expert himself but able to simplify things which might baffle anyone less knowledgeable.

'You've changed your perfume,' he said suddenly. 'That isn't *Rêve de Grasse*.'

She had dabbed some behind her ears while fetching the laptop. It pleased her that he remembered the original name of the scent the *contessa* had given her. 'This is Loulou. D'you like it?'

'Not as much as the other.'

Rebuffed, she said, 'Tom gave it to me.'

In fact it was from a sample given away with some eye make-up. As soon as the words were out she regretted the fabrication. As a rule she was never untruthful and couldn't understand why she had lied to him now. But then being with Van always had strange effects on her. It made her intensely happy and, at the same time, unhappy because his visits were brief and as soon as he'd gone away she was tormented by thoughts of all the alluring women, of the right age, he must meet when he wasn't with her.

Van made no comment, perhaps because he was concentrating, or perhaps because he was irritated. If only she could read his mind and find out what he thought about her. Was she just a girl he felt responsible for? Or did his avuncular manner mask feelings he chose to ignore?

'How is Project X going?' she asked.

It was how he always referred to the project he was working on.

'Still a few bugs to iron out.' He had never discussed it in detail.

The next time he came to Paris it was May. The end of her probationary year was on the horizon and she was impatient for the promised editorial vacancy to materialise.

'When can you get some time off?' Van asked.

'I'm not sure. Why?'

'Cousin Kate's getting married in September. She'd like you to be there. I'll take care of your travel expenses.'

Anny didn't attempt to hide the surge of joy inside her. A trip to America to meet Van's family was a treat beyond all expectations.

'I'll talk to the personnel director. Who is Kate marrying?'

'Her boss. He's a widower with two young children. Kate's loved him for years, since before he married someone else. She was resigned to staying single, then his wife became seriously ill and died just over a year ago. How Robert feels about Kate is hard to say. His primary reason may be that his children need someone in place of their mother.'

'Would she marry him on that basis?'

'I imagine she'd consider it a better option than going through the same thing again. There are plenty of women around who would jump at him.'

'Poor Kate: it must have been agony for her the first time. I can't imagine anything worse than seeing the man you love marry someone else.'

Van said, 'I think Kate would tell you a worse thing is watching someone you love losing the person they love. How about some more coffee?'

In the weeks that followed Van's visit, Anny spent a lot of time thinking over his comment about his cousin. Clearly he admired her very much. Equally clearly she deserved his admiration. By comparison Anny felt very young and inadequate. Why *should* Van love her? she asked herself. What qualities did she have to make her lovable? The answer seemed to be none.

She made up her mind to change that; to make some space in her life for helping other people as well as enjoying herself. While she was finding out about the various organisations set up to help the poor, the sick and the old, something happened almost on her own doorstep, making further enquiries unnecessary.

On a Saturday, when it was her turn to re-stock the fridge and buy fruit and salad ingredients, which was what all three girls lived on when not eating out, she was walking home with two laden carriers when an old man shuffling ahead of her tripped on an uneven paving slab and fell down.

Anny propped her shopping bags against the wall and rushed to his aid. Luckily there was a bench close by. She helped him up and supported him to it. He was not one of the local winos. Although his clothes were shabby, his manners were patrician. It turned out he lived in the same building as she did, in one of the smallest apartments on the top floor. His name was Aristide Dunois.

From then on she spent an increasing amount of her free time with him. His eyesight was poor and he could no longer read the books which lined every room of his old-fashioned home. He did not bother to cook so Anny made soups and casseroles which only needed heating up. When she felt the moment was right, she offered to do some cleaning for him.

Monsieur Dunois was nearly ninety, the same generation as the *contessa*. Once he had moved in similar circles, but now he was a recluse. His great fear was of falling ill and being put in an old people's home. He wanted to die where he was.

Anny brought Tom to see him and they had a vigorous argument about the Pompidou Centre which Tom thought exciting and Monsieur Dunois considered a desecration of the *quartier* known as the Marais. She didn't mention her new friend in her E-mails to Van, nor were Fran and Julie aware of how much time she spent with the old gentleman.

Five weeks before she was due to go to America for Kate's wedding, Monsieur Dunois caught a cold which turned to bronchitis. He refused to let Anny call a doctor.

'If it kills me, so be it. I've outlived my usefulness here. I'm ready to move on.'

He recovered, but the illness left him even more frail than before. She knew she would not be able to go to Kate's wedding. There was no one else to look after him and if he died in her absence she would never forgive herself. An affection had sprung up between them. She couldn't desert him even though it meant giving up her heart's desire, to visit America with Van.

She wrote a letter to him, explaining the situation, but put off E-mailing it until the next day. She didn't start work till ten which gave her time to go to the bakery for a croissant still warm from the oven for Aristide's breakfast. She and the others ate them only at weekends, but he needed to put on weight. His face was gaunt, his hands skeletal.

As he had breakfast in bed, she had a duplicate key to let herself in and make him a pot of camomile tea before carrying the tray to his bedroom. She found him propped up by pillows, wearing the headset she had bought him to use with audio-tapes of French classics. The curtains were open, letting in the morning sun. The bedside lamp was still alight and Aristide's chin was sunk on his chest. He was a very light sleeper, roused by the slightest disturbance. But when she put her hand on his, it felt cold and he didn't stir.

Tom went to the funeral with her. The only other person present was the old man's lawyer. Afterwards, at his request, they returned to Aristide's apartment for the reading of his will.

'Perhaps he was a miser and you are about to inherit his secret hoard,' Tom murmured, in English, as they sat in the back of the lawyer's car.

Anny shook her head. 'I'd like to have one of his books as a keepsake, but I know he was very poor. His rent ate up most of his pension. Last winter he had to sell the last of his pictures to pay the heating bills.'

Although she now had the American trip to look forward to, she felt very sad about Aristide.

His will was brief. His books and remaining furniture were to be sold, the proceeds to settle any outstanding bills and any surplus to go to the organisation called Medicine Without Frontiers. He had left a bequest to Anny: the contents of a small trunk.

Tom helped her to carry it down to the girls' apartment. When she unlocked it, he said, 'I thought it might be full of bank notes or bonds, not all that old junk.'

But later, when Tom had gone, and Anny began to sort through the mass of papers the trunk contained, she realised Aristide's legacy was of the greatest possible value to her.

Van met her flight when it landed at Kennedy Airport.

'I hadn't realised before how very French you look,' was the first thing he said.

That season everyone in Paris who had good legs, and many who hadn't, was wearing a very short skirt. Anny had searched for tights matched to her suit of deep violet wool, a practical colour that suited her better than black. Her shoes and her bag were a combination of black patent leather and pale grey suede, and round her neck she had wound a long floaty scarf, lent by the magazine's fashion editor, of palest grey silk chiffon printed in black with leopard-style spots. She knew she looked very different from her sea-urchin self of earlier years.

'Living in Paris is the best way to learn how to arrange oneself.' She gave him her hand, at the same time offering her cheek.

He kissed her on both cheeks and then, still holding her hand, inclined his tall head to brush his lips not on her knuckles as she expected but on the inside of her wrist.

The gesture, performed with the casual panache of a Frenchman, stopped Anny's breath for a moment. She almost reverted to gaucherie by letting slip a school-girlish exclamation, but managed to swallow it.

'How did you like your first transatlantic flight?'

'I loved every minute. People say what a bore flying is, but it wasn't for me. Any experience is special the first time you do it.'

As Van looked down at her, for once she could read his mind. She was ninety-nine per cent certain he was wondering if she had made love yet.

'It was extravagant of you to buy me a business-class ticket. Economy would have been fine.'

'Economy flights can be hell. I wanted this trip to be fun for you all the way.'

He had come in his father's car, a luxurious limousine which made the two-hour drive to the Carlisles' house in Connecticut seem much shorter than in a smaller, less comfortable vehicle.

Accustomed to the aggressive behaviour of Paris motorists, Anny found Van's style of driving soothingly laid-back. While his attention was on the road, she was able to indulge in a discreet but thorough study of him.

He was twenty-nine now to her nineteen and a half. The gap was narrowing. Wearing a dark blue blazer over a light blue shirt, open at the collar, with pale khaki chinos, he looked as if he had walked out of one of the 'old money, gracious living' ads in American glossies like *Town and Country* and the US edition of *Vogue*, which were read from cover to cover by the journalists on the magazine she worked for.

But he would have looked equally at home in the editorial pages of prestigious French and Italian magazines. Like other Americans she had met while working in Paris, he displayed his European heritage in his olive complexion and black hair. But whose genes had given him eyes as blue as the Madonna's robes in old master paintings or the overalls of French workmen?

The pleasure she found in looking at him after a long separation made her forget not to gaze for too long. Suddenly, the freeway being clear, Van turned his head and caught her watching him.

A year ago she would have blushed and looked quickly away. Now she had the poise to smile and say, 'Your shirt reminds me of a colour Duccio uses in his paintings. Fran's boyfriend has upgraded his PC and given her the old one, so we now have a CD-ROM drive and can browse the world's great art galleries.'

'I can't believe you spend many evenings sitting at home, holding hands with a mouse. Is Tom still in tow?'

'He's gone home and I've been too busy writing to gad about much. Just recently the most fantastic story fell right into my lap. It's so good I think it could speed up my transfer to editorial. But before I tell you about it, how's Project X going?'

'We have a launch date now. All we need is some more investment. That's not so easy to get. You'd be amazed at the number of top-level businessmen who have only the vaguest idea how the information superhighway is going to revolutionise the world in the next few decades.'

As he talked, with the fierce conviction that had long ago convinced Anny he would one day be up there with

Gates in the pantheon of men who had made major contributions to the information revolution, she wondered how much it would change him.

'So far our major investor is Emily Lancaster.'

'Who's Emily Lancaster?' asked Anny, visualising a rich American widow whose principal interest was increasing her late husband's fortune.

'She's a software engineer, British by birth but raised over here. Her grandfather was the owner of Cranmere, one of England's finest stately homes. Emily grew up under the aegis of James Gardiner. Does his name ring a bell?'

'One of the kingpins in the computer industry, isn't he?'

'That's right. Back in the early Eighties, Gardiner was known as "The Young Lion of Electronics". He's the brain behind Oz computers. He married Summer Roberts, the designer. They met when she was Emily's tutor at Cranmere.'

The smile round his mouth as he spoke of her set off Anny's mental alarm bells. But her tone was casual as she asked, 'How old is she? Where did you meet her?'

'At a computer convention. She's about the same age as I am...with much the same views about the future of cyberspace.'

'What is she like as a person?'

'You'll be meeting her at the wedding. She divides her time between Cranmere and an apartment in New York.'

Anny's heart felt like a stone dropped from a bridge into fathoms of ice-cold water. Was this aristocratic Englishwoman with her computer expertise the one who would capture Van's heart, perhaps had already captured it?

'I'll look forward to that,' she said brightly. 'But aren't you at all nervous that she might accidentally leak your ideas to James Gardiner who has the funds to make use of them before you can?'

'Gardiner doesn't need to pirate other men's brain-children. He has plenty of his own. But anyway Emily isn't privy to our secrets.'

'If she doesn't know what the project is, how have you persuaded her to invest in it?'

'She knows me and believes I'm capable of the same kind of breakthrough her uncle achieved.'

She's in love with you, Anny thought glumly. 'Does she work for him?' she asked.

'No, she has her own company, Emel. Its most popular product is Dresscode, a database for clothes and accessories. It comes in several forms. There's a complex version used by the costume departments of theatrical and ballet companies and a simple one to help women allocate their clothes budget, work out cost-per-wear and so on.'

'Sounds a good idea.'

'After you've met she'll probably send you a copy. What's this fantastic story you mentioned?'

'I made friends with an old man in one of the other apartments. He called himself Aristide Dunois. Nobody knew his real name was Prince Guy Aristide Dunois de Guermantes and that during World War Two he was a Resistance fighter, one of the "people of the night" with a price on his head.'

'Have you persuaded him to disclose his real identity?'

'No, but he knew I was itching to become a staff journalist. When he died, a few weeks ago, he left me a trunk containing all his private papers, with a letter giving me permission to use them in any way I liked. He had a fascinating life before he fell on hard times. I've written a profile of him. It's being considered now. I'm hoping that when I get back they'll have decided to use it.'

'Did you bring a copy with you? I'd like to read it.'

'I'd rather you read it in print under my byline.'

'What about illustrations? Will they be able to find old photographs of him?'

'I've supplied some with the text. The trunk contained several albums. There's one particularly good shot of him on a Côte d'Azur beach in 1924 when sunbathing was the in thing to do. He's with a lot of other leading lights of the Twenties. He was terribly handsome.'

Van took his eyes off the road to give her a quizzical look. 'It sounds as if you've fallen in love with your subject.'

'I should think a lot of women loved him when he was young. But his dashing looks didn't last into old age.'

'Is there enough material for a biography?' Van asked.

'I hadn't thought of that. I think there might be. But a book takes a lot more effort than an article. I'm not sure I could do it.'

'Of course you could,' Van said emphatically. 'If the subject matter is there, it's merely a question of disciplining yourself to write a few pages or so many words every day.'

'Easier said than done, especially if I'm working flat out as a staff writer.'

'You'll have to cut down on your social life,' was Van's somewhat acid comment. 'If dating is more important to you than getting ahead, so be it. But nothing worthwhile was ever achieved without sweat and sacrifice. It's possible that when the profile comes out you'll be approached by some publishers. The story of a blue-blooded war hero who died in obscurity has a lot of appeal. What about his love life?'

'He had three wives...not because he was fickle but

because they all died. His first wife was in his Resistance group. She got caught and sent to a concentration camp. His second wife died having a stillborn baby. His last love was a French actress, already incurably ill when he met her. They had less than a year together.'

'Sounds to me as if the contents of that trunk could earn you a lot of money,' said Van. 'Get hold of some first-class biographies to see how it's done before you start. I can lend you a couple of good ones.'

His confidence in her ability to cope with such an ambitious venture was warming.

With this new possibility opening up, the expectation of a step up the career ladder awaiting her return to Paris and, starting now, an exciting holiday in the company of the man she loved, she should have felt on top of the world.

As indeed she would have done had Van not told her about Emily Lancaster.

# CHAPTER SIX

Two days later, after breakfast on the morning of Kate's wedding, Anny went up to her bedroom to change for the ceremony. It was being held in the Carlisle family mansion because Kate's parents were dead.

While most people staying in the house were still in bed, florists had started transforming the living room, dining room and hall. Now a stylist from the best salon in Hartford had arrived to do the bride's and several other ladies' hair. Caterers were laying places for sixty people to sit down to a five-course luncheon at two long tables at right angles to the top table.

Anny felt overwhelmed by the luxurious standard of living Van's relations enjoyed. She had known they were rich, but the reality of their riches was so different from the threadbare grandeur of the *palazzo* that she couldn't quite adjust to it. Here there was nothing shabby. Even the antique furniture, although authentic period pieces, had had all trace of wear or damage removed by skilled restorers.

As she had declined the services of the stylist, preferring to do her hair herself, she went downstairs ahead of time, hoping to spend a quiet hour in Mr Carlisle's library which he had shown her on the night of her arrival.

When she opened the door, expecting to find the room empty, a haven from the bustle going on elsewhere, Van and his father were there.

'Oh...I'm sorry...I should have knocked...'

Before she could back out both men rose. 'Don't run

away, my dear,' said Mr Carlisle. 'We were only passing the time. Allow me to say you look charming.'

'Thank you.'

While his father was speaking, Van had come to where she was standing. He removed her hand from the doorknob, drawing her into the room and closing the door behind her.

'I second that,' he said, smiling down at her.

The wedding was informal with the men wearing lounge suits. As she had never seen him in a suit before, she was dazzled by Van's masculine elegance in perfectly tailored lightweight grey worsted with a finely striped blue-on-white shirt and a silk tie the colour of lapis lazuli. A white carnation was tucked in his buttonhole and a navy-spotted claret silk handkerchief overflowed his breast pocket. He looked every inch what the French called an *homme du mond*, meaning a man of the world with a special air of distinction.

'I'll go rustle up some coffee,' said Mr Carlisle. 'Failing that, it's never too early for a glass of champagne.' He left the room.

'That dress is the essence of chic,' said Van, still holding her hand and appraising her outfit as they moved towards the window with its view of immaculate lawns and well-tended borders.

'It's nice of you to say so, but I think all your female relations will recognise its humble origins. This is a mass-produced cheapie. It won't compare very well with designer numbers.'

'My male relations don't know designer from thrift shop,' Van said dryly. 'They'll be looking at the figures inside the dresses. You'll be right out in front of the competition on that count.'

The compliment was accompanied by another appraisal, this time of the curves above and below her slim waist cinched by a wide shaped belt exactly matching the softly clinging grey chiffon, its colour matching her eyes.

He had not looked at her in this way since she modelled the dress he had said made her look like a mermaid. Then he lifted her hand and, instead of kissing it in the usual way, pressed his lips to the delicate skin over her pulse.

The intimate sensuality of the caress was as unexpected and unnerving as a seismic shock wave. A moment later it was over. He had released her hand and was waiting for her to sit down in the chair vacated by his father. Trying to maintain an appearance of composure while thrills were still running up her arm and her heart was behaving like a Geiger counter measuring maximum intensity, she sank into the deep leather chair.

'So...what do you make of the American side of my family?' he asked, relaxing in the other chair.

'I feel a bit out of my depth,' she admitted. If the touch of his lips on her wrist had such a shattering effect, what would happen if he kissed her on the mouth?

'Don't you mean high and dry?' he said, smiling. 'A mermaid can never be out of her depth.' Before she could answer, he went on, 'That's the way I feel too. I like my father, but when I was small I hardly ever saw him. We didn't play games together. He didn't shape my ideas. There's not the strong bond between us that you have with Bart and I'd like to have with my children. The only place I felt I belonged was at Orengo.'

'When will you be there again?'

'I'm not sure. There's some sorting out still to do, but it's hard to get away right now. When's the next time Bart will be there?'

'Next month probably. I hope I can get some more time off to go down and see him. You know how it is with him...always a bit of a worry.'

'I know, but don't worry today. Don't let anything spoil the wedding for you.'

Did he but know it, his advice rekindled the other worry which had been weighing on her mind since the day of her arrival. From the moment he came towards her, looking so dashing, she had temporarily forgotten the existence of his other guest, the one whose arrival might dash her hopes for ever.

But would he have kissed her wrist in that tender, erotic way if Emily Lancaster was the woman he wanted?

The door opened and Mrs Carlisle came in.

'Do you know where your father is, Van?' she asked, as he stood up.

'He went to see about coffee.'

He did not compliment his stepmother on her outfit, Anny noticed. It was rather over the top. Tricia Carlisle must have been exceptionally pretty as a girl. But now, in her middle fifties, her face was becoming the mask of a woman who couldn't accept that youth was behind her. Her elaborate hairstyle, her dress, her long scarlet nails and her rings all advertised her status as a woman who could spend hours and thousands of dollars on her appearance. It was impossible to imagine her in a kitchen or gardening apron, her hair even slightly dishevelled, a smudge of flour or soil on her cheek.

'I could do with a glass of champagne. Organise it, will you, dear?'

As Van left, she took his place, her heavily made up green eyes noting the details of Anny's appearance.

'Kate has been in a dream since they announced their engagement. If I hadn't taken charge, I don't know what would have happened.' She glanced at her expensive gold and diamond watch. 'Alida and Guido will be arriving soon. They're coming from New York and spending tonight at the country club. You haven't met Van's mother, have you?'

Anny shook her head. She had been surprised to hear that Edward Carlisle's first wife and her second husband would be among the guests. But perhaps in a culture where divorce and re-marriage was commonplace, the meeting of current wives and ex-wives was not the social dynamite it would be in France where a blind eye was turned to amours provided they didn't disrupt family life.

'Kate invited her,' said Tricia. 'I didn't think she would come, but perhaps she has heard an intriguing rumour that Project X is not her son's only obsession.' After a pause, she added, 'Alida is very Italian. She and Edward are opposite poles. Van is the strangest mixture of her emotional temperament and his father's shrewdness and discretion. As you've mixed with a lot of Continentals, I'm sure you'll get on with her.'

At this point the men returned, Van carrying a tray with a coffee pot on it and his father bearing a bottle in an ice bucket.

Anny's thoughts were in a whirl. What had Tricia meant by that remark about an intriguing rumour? What or who was Van's other obsession? Was he suspected of being in love with Emily Lancaster? Had the kiss on her wrist a short while ago been merely the Italian in him performing an impulsive gallantry, one which it wouldn't occur to him she might take seriously?

The library had a drinks cupboard stocked with glasses including crystal flutes. After half a glass of champagne, Anny found it easier to look as if she were enjoying herself. But she couldn't help wishing they were on the deck of *Sea Dreams*, drinking Spanish *cava* from cheap glasses bought from a market.

The journalist in her found being with these people interesting in the same way that a zoologist could spend hours studying a group of animals. But in her private persona she knew this wasn't her sphere. It couldn't compare with Orengo with its wild, tangled garden and damp-spotted looking glasses reflecting deserted rooms filled with shadowy golden light diffused by the peeling shutters.

The windows at the far end of the library overlooked the drive. Presently a limousine could be seen arriving.

'That will be your mother, Van. You say hello to her first and then bring her here,' Tricia instructed. 'We have at least half an hour before the others start arriving.'

To Anny's surprise, Van took her glass from her hand and put it on the small table beside her chair. 'Come and meet my other parent.'

In the corridor outside the library, she said, 'Don't you want to have a little time alone with your mother?'

He was holding her lightly by the elbow, the touch of his cool, strong fingers sending a current of pleasure up her arm.

'Because you never knew your parents, you have a lot of illusions about family ties and family life. My family's relationships aren't the way you imagine them. We sometimes come together for rites of passage like weddings, then we go our separate ways again.'

'But Tricia said—' She stopped short.

'What did Tricia say?'

'That your mother was very fond of you,' she improvised.

'Tricia claims to be fond of her children. I suspect it's only as long as they behave in the way she wants them to…being a credit to her,' he said cynically.

They heard the front door bell ringing. One of the white-overalled helpers appeared from the other side of the spacious hall, saw them and went away.

When Van opened the door, a couple were standing in the imposing open porch with its two carved stone benches today ranged with baskets of white and yellow carnations.

'Giovanni!' The woman surged forward to embrace him.

'Good to see you, Mamma.' Van stooped so that she could kiss him, then extended a hand to her companion. *'Ciao, Guido. Come va?'*

His stepfather wrung his hand and clapped him on the shoulder. He was a head shorter than Van and of a burlier build.

'Mamma, this is Annette Howard.'

'I am delighted to meet you. Kate calls you "Giovanni's mermaid". You have known each other since you were children, I believe?'

'I was a child when we met. Giovanni was almost grown-up.' Anny used his full name in deference to his mother's preference for it.

'Please...don't remind me how old he is. It makes me feel middle-aged. Of course I was very young when he was born, but even so one prefers not to count the years. This is my husband. We also knew each other in our youth, but it was many years later that we came together.'

Guido bowed over Anny's hand. When Van explained that their hosts were waiting for them in the library, he and his mother went ahead and his stepfather walked with Anny, responding to her enquiries about their journey. His command of English was not as good as his wife's. When he discovered that Anny spoke Italian, his face lit up with relief that there was somebody present with whom he could converse in his own language.

From then, when it wasn't discourteous, he seized every chance to chat to her. Anny didn't mind being monopolised. Even though, when the other guests started arriving, they all took the trouble to seek her out and be nice to her, like Guido she felt an outsider in a large family group.

Almost the last to arrive was the other outsider, Emily Lancaster. By then the Carlisles were stationed in the hall, receiving, and the house was full of people drinking champagne and circulating, or admiring the display of wedding presents in the large room where the family watched television.

With Guido beside her, Anny was near the foot of the flower-garlanded oak-panelled staircase when a striking woman with a cloud of red hair came through the open front door to shake hands with the Carlisles.

She was wearing a very simple ankle-length dress of pale green jersey, the colour of asparagus stalks, with several long ropes of jade beads. As she stood talking to her hosts, Van came out of the living room, moving swiftly towards her. Clearly he had been watching for her arrival and was delighted to see her.

Equally clearly the pleasure was mutual. She sensed him coming and turned, her lovely face lighting with gladness.

Watching them embrace, Anny felt all her hopes crumbling to dust. They looked right together. No wonder they were the subject of an 'intriguing rumour'. She turned back to Guido, asking him if he knew any of the ports in southern Italy which she and Bart had visited in their meanderings.

Guido did not. A son of the prosperous north, he had a low regard for the poorer regions of his country. Extolling the beauty of the Italian lakes, suddenly he stopped short. At the same moment Anny felt a touch on her arm. Turning her head, she found Van and the redhead beside them.

'Emily, I'd like you to meet my friend Anny Howard and my stepfather Guido Rossi. Lady Emily is English but has spent a lot of her life in the States,' he explained, for Guido's benefit.

If they had met somewhere else, knowing nothing about each other, Anny knew she would have taken an instant liking to the other woman. Her freckled face and the warmth of her smile were irresistibly charming.

They had only a few minutes' conversation before it was time for everyone to find their places in the rows of identical gilt chairs, provided by the caterers, set out in the so-called living room, actually a room designed to accommodate large social gatherings.

The Rossis were in the front row with Tricia Carlisle, the bridegroom's parents and other important guests.

Anny's place was in the second row, next to Van with Emily on his other side. Music chosen by the bridal couple and recorded was playing softly as a background to the buzz of conversation. When the volume of the music rose, people lowered their voices but did not stop talking altogether until those with the best view of the staircase saw the bride and her two attendants appear round the bend in the stairs.

At the foot of the stairs, her uncle was waiting to offer her his arm. Soon everyone could see them, advancing slowly along the aisle to join the bridegroom and the minister conducting the service.

Because he was a head taller than most of the people around him, Van was among those who received a smile from the bride as she passed.

Of all the women he knew, Kate and the two women watching her from either side of him were the three he liked best. They had little in common with each other, but all had strong links with him.

Towards two of them, his feelings were fraternal. The other one occupied most of his thoughts not centred on his work. He wanted her with increasing impatience but knew the time wasn't right. As yet he had nothing to offer her.

Soon, if his hopes were realised, and he was confident they would be, he would be able to hand her the moon on a plate. Not that she would want it. His mother and stepmother and most of his other relations, with the honourable exception of Kate, were acquisitive status-seekers, women defined by their husbands' standing and by their worldly possessions.

His future wife wasn't their kind of woman. Her values were not their values. She could stand on her own feet. She shared his view of the world. This wedding was not an occasion she would greatly enjoy, but it had been an opportunity to spend a little time with her at a stage of his life when he couldn't see her as often as he wanted.

When the service came to the point when the bridal couple were exchanging their vows and some of the women present were beginning to sniff and fumble for handkerchiefs, he glanced down at her rapt face. Engrossed in the ceremony, she seemed unaware he was watching her. He wondered if she had any idea how much he wanted her.

Not wanting her to look up and catch him with his feelings revealed, he looked at his other guest. She was equally intent. Perhaps all women identified with the bride on these occasions.

Men's minds were differently geared. Some of them would be looking forward to some more of the vintage champagne his father had laid on. Those not happily married would be pitying the bridegroom for putting his head in the noose a second time. Others who, like himself, were tired of being bachelors, would be envying Robert the pleasures of his honeymoon.

As he watched Kate and Robert exchange their first married kiss, Van felt a powerful impulse to let his heart rule his head by declaring his feelings immediately and sweeping his love off somewhere for an unofficial honeymoon.

As the bridal couple disappeared in the direction of the hall where the guests would file past to offer congratulations, Anny decided that, at some point before their departure for the airport at Hartford, she must manage to catch Kate alone and ask her to explain the 'intriguing rumour'. If it was what she thought it must be, she would rather have it confirmed than live in agonised suspense until the public announcement.

At the luncheon, she found the wedding seating repeated, except that Van was on the end of the table with Emily and herself opposite each other. Next to Emily was an elderly man with his wife beside him and Anny had a similar couple next to her. As the two couples knew each other, they talked among themselves about golf and bridge, leaving the trio at the end to do the same on other topics.

'The last wedding I went to was in Florida,' said Emily. Speaking to Anny, she went on, 'When I arrived in America, I was thirteen. My tutor and I lived in a lovely house called *Dance of the Sun* on the Gulf Coast of Florida. There was a swimming pool and all sorts of other luxuries we hadn't been used to in England. The pool was cleaned by a guy called Skip and I fell madly in love with him. I stayed that way for a long time. But eventually it wore off and last year he asked Summer and me to his wedding. Summer being my ex-tutor. As she's married to my uncle now, we still see a lot of each other.'

'D'you think first love always wears off?' Van asked her.

'How can it not? A thirteen-year-old's ideal is light years away from the man she would choose at my age.

Skip looked like a blond Tarzan, swam like a dolphin and was a really sweet guy. But he didn't have any ambitions beyond joining the family business. After a while I realised what he needed was a small-town girl whose idea of a good time was a barbecue with the neighbours. I'm not knocking people like that. But it's not the right life for me.'

She then stopped talking about herself and drew Anny out about her career and ambitions, listening to her answers with unmistakably genuine interest.

Anny already knew that Emily was staying for the dance. Like several other guests, she was overnighting at the country club founded by one of Van's ancestors and, on occasions such as this, used by various prominent local families as an annexe to their houses.

Their conversation was brought to an end by the speeches for which many people turned their chairs towards the top table. Welcoming the guests, Mr Carlisle mentioned that they included two from Italy and 'Lady Emily Lancaster from England'.

Glancing at her as he said this, Anny knew intuitively that Emily didn't like being singled out because of her title and preferred to be known for her own achievements rather than those of her ancestors.

Anny turned her attention to the bride who had chosen not to wear white. Kate's long dress was a very pale green patterned with sprays of mimosa and her off-the-face hat was made from sprays of mimosa sent from a shop in Paris which specialised in exquisite silk imitation flowers.

She wasn't a pretty woman but her face reflected the warmth of her nature and today she was lit up by happiness. Watching her as she listened to Robert replying to the toast to the bridal couple, Anny wondered if she had the moral fibre to bear up as bravely as Kate had if the same thing happened to her and Van married someone else, more than likely the elegant redhead on the other side of the table.

After the speeches and the cake-cutting ceremony, everyone left the dining room to return to the living room where the gilt chairs had been removed, or they went outside to admire the garden while the bride was changing into her going-away clothes. At Kate's wish, the usual time-consuming group wedding photographs had been waived in favour of a video taken by a friend who was a professional photographer.

Leaving Van and Emily together, Anny excused herself to go to her room. She did spend a few minutes there, brushing her teeth—the pudding had been a death-by-meringue bombe—and retouching her lipstick. But her purpose in coming upstairs was to talk to Kate.

Before she left her bedroom, she spent a few minutes at the window watching people strolling along the paths and sitting on the seat encircling the trunk of a large tree.

As she watched, Van and Emily appeared from the end of a pergola. Her gestures suggested she was telling him a funny story. Moments later he threw back his head and laughed. They looked very good together. A perfect match, she thought dully. Was there any point in asking Kate to explain the 'intriguing rumour'? Wasn't the answer self-evident?

All the same she went to Kate's room. The door was closed and the murmur of voices from within put her off knocking. What she wanted to know couldn't be asked in front of other people and probably Kate's two close friends who were acting as her attendants would stay with her till she was ready.

At four o'clock the newly-weds left in Robert's car. They were honeymooning on Cape Cod in a friend's summer cottage. When they had been waved on their way, tea and wedding cake was served in the garden.

About five the guests began to leave, most of them to reconvene at the dance a few hours later.

On returning downstairs, Anny had been waylaid by Guido who confided that he found it tiring to be surrounded by strangers, none of whom spoke his language.

'Weddings in Italy are more emotional,' he told her. 'When the bridegroom leaves, his mother breaks down and all her friends sob in sympathy.'

There was a twinkle in his eye which made Anny laugh and say, 'I'm sure you're exaggerating.'

'Only a little. In my country we don't have your "stiff upper lip". We show our feelings. Who is the girl with red hair I see deep in conversation with Alida's son?'

The question surprised her. Surely any rumour reaching his wife's ears would have been discussed with him?

She told him who Emily was, adding, 'She's also a computer expert. I expect they're discussing developments on the Internet.'

At this point they were joined by Signora Rossi who asked him to dispose of her teacup. 'And find someone else to talk to, *caro*, because I want a tête-à-tête with Annette.' As soon as he was out of earshot, she said, 'Guido didn't want to come. He is very jealous of my first husband, which is foolish, but Italian men are like that. They are passionate and possessive. Giovanni will be just the same when he marries. Here, among his American relations, he behaves as they do. But inside—' she placed her hand on her chest '—he is more hot-blooded than he shows…and very macho. But you have known him a long time. You understand what he's like.'

Anny said, 'I'm not sure that I do. He seems to me very "New World". I don't feel this is his milieu—' with a gesture embracing their surroundings '—but the spirit that opened up the West and put the first man on the moon, that's very strong in Van…Giovanni.'

'Perhaps you are right. I don't understand his work.

Computers are a mystery to me. I know it's very important to him, but not so important that he will neglect his wife as his father neglected me. Edward's career always came first. American women don't mind that. They want their husbands to be important men. But I wanted only to be loved.'

Thinking of Kate, Anny said, 'Some American women are incredibly loving. Can one ever generalise about people? You mentioned that you knew Guido when you were both very young. What happened to keep you apart?'

'My parents didn't approve of him,' Alida said, with a shrug. 'Guido's family were industrialists. My father was also a self-made man but my mother never forgot her father was a count. She wanted me to make an important marriage. When she found out Edward was descended from the early colonists, she encouraged him to court me. I thought an American diplomat was more exciting than a boy I had known all my life. I was eighteen and Edward was thirty-four. It was a recipe for disaster. Here comes Giovanni.'

When he joined them, Van said, 'I'm taking Emily to the club, Mamma. She wants to relax with a book for a couple of hours. How about you and Guido? Would you also like to leave now?'

'Yes, please. I must also rest,' said his mother. 'We will see you later, Annette.'

For a few minutes before it was time to go down and join the others for the drive to the country club, Anny stood in front of the long mirror in her bedroom, examining her reflection.

She was wearing the *contessa*'s dévoré velvet dress and the shop which had supplied the mimosa for Kate's wedding hat had made her a spray of silk-velvet flowers attached to a comb now fixed in her upswept hair. She was not wearing any jewellery. The dress didn't need a necklace and it would have been vandalism to pierce the exquisite material with a brooch. She had had her ears pierced in Spain when she was sixteen but didn't possess any earrings worthy of the dress.

A knock at the door startled her. Could it be Mrs Carlisle?

'Come in.'

Van walked into the bedroom. She had thought he looked wonderful in a suit. In black tie, he took her breath away. Somehow she had never thought of him owning a white dinner jacket like the ones worn by people partying on the enormous yachts she had sometimes seen berthed in places frequented by the very rich.

'I assumed you'd be wearing that dress,' he said. 'I saw these in New York and thought they would go with it.'

From his pocket he took a small black leather box and opened it to show her the contents. The two pieces of precious stone resting on the dark blue satin lining reminded her of how the sea looked when the sun was shining and the sea-bed was sandy.

'Aquamarines! Oh, Van...they're beautiful.'

'Try them on. See how they look.'

Excitement made her fingers clumsy. She couldn't find the tiny holes in her lobes.

'Here, let me do it,' said Van.

His fingers were steady. Moments later the earrings were in place, the slender pins held by tiny gold butterflies. After studying the effect, he said, 'They suit you. I was keeping them for your next birthday, but I may not be able to get over for it and tonight seems a good time to wear them.'

She turned to see her reflection, then looked up at him, her eyes shining. 'They're perfect...gorgeous. But what an extravagance! They must have cost you the earth.'

The quirk at the corner of his mouth made her realise the naiveté of her comment. Emily would never have blurted out that remark.

Trying to retrieve some poise, she said. 'I've often admired aquamarines in jewellers' shop windows. I never expected to wear any. Thank you.'

Putting one hand on his chest to steady herself, she stood on tiptoe to brush a light kiss on his cheek.

What happened next was totally unexpected.

Van put his hands on her waist, inclining his head in the instinctive response she had seen him make many times since the guests started arriving; even the tallest women being unable to kiss him without his co-operation.

Against her lips she felt the taut skin of his face between cheekbone and jawline, its texture smooth from recent shaving yet unlike the feel of her own face. He smelt faintly of soap or shaving lotion: a scent as subtle and fresh as the tang of sea air.

And then, as she thought the moment of bliss was over and was about to lower her heels to the floor, something seemed to ignite between them like spontaneous combustion.

Suddenly, she was in his arms and he was kissing her mouth.

# CHAPTER SEVEN

'I DIDN'T intend to do that.'

Anny, her eyes still closed, her mind a blank, only her senses functioning, was brought down to earth by a husky murmur quite unlike Van's usual voice.

Opening her eyes, she looked into his. As what he had said got through to her, she said, her own voice a breathless murmur, 'But you did…and I liked it.'

'Your lipstick is smudged. You'd better do something about it. We're due to leave very soon. I'll see you downstairs.'

Van put her away from him. Then he turned and strode out of the bedroom, closing the door behind him.

On his way to his room, Van cursed himself for succumbing to impulse. But she had looked so irresistibly beautiful in the glamorous Twenties dress and his earrings.

In his bathroom, he took some tissues from a holder fixed to the wall by the handbasin. The soap-on-a-rope in the shower was still wet from his second shower of the day. He made a pad of the tissues, rubbed it over the soap and then scrubbed the traces of colour from his lips.

He scowled at himself in the mirror. It had been a bad idea to go to her room. He should have known better. It had been clear for some time that Anny thought herself in love with him. But as Emily had said at lunch, referring to her own calf love, the chances were that she would grow out of it.

He was past those ephemeral emotions that blazed up

but swiftly burned out. He needed a woman in his life, but on a permanent basis and Anny wasn't ready for permanence yet. It might be four or five years before she was fully mature, ready to make the kind of commitment he wanted from a woman.

Why in hell's name couldn't he feel this way about Emily? They had everything two people needed to make a strong, lasting partnership. Except that she wasn't in love with him, nor he with her.

It was Anny he wanted: but not Anny as she was now. Anny grown-up, her character fully formed, her sights fixed on different achievements from the things she was set on now.

Van returned to the bedroom and filled a glass with iced water from the vacuum flask on the night table, replenished every evening when the beds were turned down. He drank it, knowing that it would take more than a cold drink to douse the desire her soft, warm lips had aroused. A cold shower would be more effective but there wasn't time for one now. And later, God help him, he was going to have to dance with her at least once. There was no way out of that without wounding her feelings, the last thing he wanted to do.

God! What a situation. Why weren't you born five years earlier, Anny, my darling? How am I going to hold out?

When Anny went down to the hall, only Van's father was there.

She could see that, by comparison with her low-key look at the wedding, the way she was dressed tonight surprised him in the same way that it surprised her that this somewhat staid older man had none of the dynamic vitality which characterised his son.

They had been chatting for only a few minutes when other house guests joined them. Van's parents employed a chauffeur who looked after several cars belonging to the household. He drove some of the guests to the club, Mr Carlisle took his wife and two others and Van drove the third car, with two people in the back and Anny sitting beside him.

She was silent during the drive, certain now that her earlier worries about Van being in love with Emily had no foundation. Had it been so, he would never have kissed her: he wasn't the kind of man to play fast and loose, as Bart put it, and the embrace in her bedroom had had nothing fraternal about it. It had been the most passionate kiss she had ever exchanged.

Thinking about it made her tremble with longing to repeat it. What was he thinking and feeling? she wondered, shooting a sideways glance at the strong profile illumined by the glow from the car's headlights.

The fact that he had walked out of her bedroom immediately afterwards didn't deflate her. She felt that what had happened had taken them both by surprise and, because of the timing, there had been nothing else he could do. But surely, during the dance, there would be an opportunity for them to slip away and find a secluded place in the grounds of the club to kiss again, and to talk about this sudden change in their relationship. Well, not sudden on her side because she had wanted him to kiss her for a long time. But perhaps it was only tonight that Van had realised she was ready for love.

The country club had once been a large private house in whose grounds there was now an eighteen-hole golf course and many other sporting facilities.

A large private room had been reserved for the Carlisles' party, with dancing to a small live group taking place in what had once been a very large conservatory adjoining the supper room.

Because Van and Anny and Emily were among the youngest people present and most of the guests were much older, it was clear that the group would be playing mainly cheek-to-cheek music.

Anny loved to dance and had been to some discos in Paris where the music was wild and she had responded to the rhythms with an energetic abandon which had startled the more inhibited Tom.

Tonight, however, neither her dress nor her mood was right for that sort of dancing. She wanted the music to be slow and sweet so that Van would be able to hold her close to him.

Shortly after their arrival, Emily appeared, her arresting colouring set off by a black satin shirt and a full skirt matched to her hair. Tonight she was wearing a triple-strand choker of polished amber beads, an adaptation of the conventional pearl choker which picked up the amber glints in her striking hazel eyes.

'Anny, you look ravishing!' she exclaimed warmly. 'What a marvellous dress. Where did you find it?'

When its source had been explained to her, she said, 'I must have a picture of it to send to Summer. She's mad about lovely textiles. I'll fetch my camera.'

She was back within a few minutes and whisked Anny off to another of the public rooms, not in use that evening, where she could pose without attracting attention.

'Come with us, Van,' she commanded. 'I don't have a good picture of you to pin up in the gallery of friends on the wall of my workroom at Cranmere.

'This is a sort of library-cum-music room. I had some more tea in here when I got back this afternoon,' she said, as she opened the door and switched on the lights.

The room had a wall of books, a grand piano, and many comfortable slip-covered chairs and sofas.

Emily was clearly an experienced photographer and had already worked out where and how she wanted Anny to pose. Her incisive directions reduced Anny's camera-shyness, which she wouldn't have felt at all if Van hadn't been there, watching the proceedings.

After taking several shots, one of them with Anny standing close to an ornate mirror, Emily said, 'Now let's have a shot of you both leaning against the piano with that big vase of flowers in the background. Then, when you're both famous names, I can sell it for exorbitant fees to magazines,' she added mischievously.

'Not if you want to stay friends with us,' Van told her dryly. 'Close to the top of my wish list is keeping my privacy. Letting the press invade their lives may be necessary for showbiz people, but my life is going to stay private.'

'Don't worry: I was only joking. Stand a bit closer, will you? That's fine...perfect. Now just one more shot of Anny sitting on the piano with her legs crossed. Lift her onto it, will you, Van?'

'I don't think I ought to sit on it. I might damage it,' Anny objected.

'Nonsense...your light weight won't hurt it,' Emily assured her. 'It will make a terrific picture.'

Gripping her waist more firmly than he had earlier, Van swung Anny onto the piano, then stepped away.

'Lean back on your hands, cross your legs and think Marlene Dietrich,' Emily instructed.

Anny did as she was told, the slit at the side of her skirt falling open to show her slender legs in sheer hose and the shoes with silver kid heels made for the dress. Obeying Emily's final instruction, she focussed on Van, half-closed her eyelids and gave him a come-hither look.

She thought he would laugh, but in fact he looked curiously wooden and unamused. But Emily was delighted. 'You're a natural model, Anny. OK, you can lift her down, Van. We'd better get back to the party.'

Anny could have slid to the floor unaided, but she waited for him to assist her, leaning forward to place her hands on his shoulders and smiling into his eyes as he took hold of her waist. At the same moment, Emily stepped to one side and took her final shot of Van in the act of lifting Anny's one hundred and twenty-five pounds as easily as if she had still been the skinny nine-year-old of their first encounter in the belvedere.

'Thank you.' She let her hands slide down his chest. His kiss had given her a confidence she had never had before, at least not with him.

Van turned away. 'If you'll give me your key, I'll take your camera back to your room for you,' he said to Emily.

'That's very sweet of you.' She handed over the camera and took her key from her small cylindrical bag. 'Turn right at the top of the stairs and my room is on the right through the second set of fire doors.

'I do like a man with nice manners,' she said to Anny, as they made their way back to the party. 'So many guys are afraid to be chivalrous now in case they get told off or snubbed. But I shouldn't think Van ever has his gestures rejected. Attractive men can get away with anything…even opening doors for hard-line feminists. It's the timid types who get blasted.'

'When you have that roll of film developed, would you send me a set of duplicates of the prints Van and I are in, please?'

'But of course…I'll send you both a set.'

Anny had to wait for an hour before Van asked her to dance. She had an intuitive feeling he had deliberately postponed the moment she had been longing for. He had danced with his mother and stepmother and with Emily and several others before he approached her and, his manner curiously formal, asked her if she would dance with him.

Van escorted her to the conservatory where about a

dozen couples had stayed on the floor since the last pause in the music. She went into his arms with the certainty that, for the rest of her life, she would remember this music, even though she had never heard it before and didn't know what it was called.

'Nice party,' he said.

It was the same remark two other men had made to her. They had been strangers making small-talk. She didn't expect this from Van.

'Do you think so?' she said, glancing up at him.

He looked surprised. 'Don't you?'

She said, 'No, I wouldn't call it "nice". That's such a lukewarm word. I would describe this party as outstanding, sensational, stupendous...the best party of my whole life. But that's because of what happened before the party...after you gave me my present.'

'That's something we have to talk about...after this dance.'

'Why not now, while we're dancing?'

'Because what I have to say may not please you,' said Van. 'If you're going to throw something at me, I'd prefer that you did it in private.'

'I've never yet thrown anything at you,' she pointed out, moving closer to him.

'There's always a first time.' He held her away by slightly raising the arm supporting her forearm and pushing against her hand with the flat of his hand. 'You've done your Dietrich act, Anny. Stop playing the seductress. It doesn't come naturally to you.'

'It might...if I had more practice. My problem is there's only one man I'd like to seduce. You.'

'In view of the gap in our ages, it's I who would be seen as the seducer. It's not a role that appeals to me.'

'Would you rather someone else seduced me?'

'I would rather you stopped talking nonsense,' he said repressively.

'Why is it nonsense? Plenty of people have indicated that they'd like to take me to bed. I can't resist them indefinitely. There's the curiosity factor, the feeling of being excluded. Why should I be left out?'

'Because you are not a lemming. You have too much intelligence to try something merely because other people are doing it. You wouldn't try cocaine, would you?'

'That's not a fair comparison. Coke can ruin people's lives.'

'So can sex,' he said grimly.

'Oh, Van...loosen up. That's a one-night stand with a stranger...completely different from a relationship with someone you know and trust. If you weren't fond of me, why did you spend the earth on these glorious earrings...why did you kiss me?'

He looked down at her. 'I've been giving you birthday presents since you were eleven...of course I'm fond of you. The kiss was a mistake...an impulse I should have controlled.'

When she couldn't conceal the pain this brusque statement caused her, his expression became exasperated. 'For God's sake, Anny, you know basic biology. I spelt all this out for you years ago, on the trip to Minorca when that Spanish boy made a pass. Do you think those same urges aren't felt by adult males? You know better than that. Any man without a woman in his life feels...keyed up sometimes.'

His black eyebrows drew together in a forbidding scowl. 'I guess most of the men you've been dancing with tonight, including some of the husbands, would have felt the same impulse if you'd been standing close with no one else around. It's almost a standard male reflex. We all get turned on by a pretty woman. Most of the time we tell ourselves, "Down, boy!" This time, foolishly, I didn't.'

She didn't like what she was hearing, and she wasn't convinced it was true.

Knowing she was being mulish, but unable to help herself, she said in a challenging tone, 'If you turn me on and I turn you on, why can't we do something about it?'

For a moment his exasperation flared into visible anger. His mouth became a hard line, his eyes looked so fierce that, had it been anyone else, she would have instinctively stepped back. Even with him she flinched from the glimpse of the furious reaction her provocative answer had aroused.

It was only a glimpse. Almost at once he masked it, saying coldly, 'Because being turned on isn't enough. People who run their lives on that basis never amount to much. Making love was meant to be more important than a roll in the hay.'

Perhaps he could see he was hurting her. His expression softened a little. 'Trust me, Anny. That's not a good route for anyone...man or woman. What happened was my fault and I'm sorry about it. It doesn't have to change things. Right now the most important thing for both of us is our work. I have to get Project X off the ground and you have to get your career in orbit.'

It was, she realised, an oblique ultimation. She wasn't going to get anywhere by arguing with him. If she persisted, it would only make matters worse.

What was behind his attitude she wasn't sure. Later, unable to sleep, she had a horrible feeling that the reason he had been 'keyed up', as he put it, was because of Emily's presence. Perhaps he was holding off from kissing her until he had more to offer her and, somehow, Anny's thank-you kiss had triggered the desire he felt for Emily.

This theory had a number of holes in it but it was the only one she could come up with. Anyway, whatever lay behind the humiliating set-down on the dance floor, it was plain that her dearest dreams were not about to be realised yet, if ever.

The rest of her time in America was a depressing anti-climax. Van made sure they were never alone together. Instead of driving her back to New York, he arranged for her to fly there on the shuttle from Hartford. Even on the short drive to that airport, they had Emily with them. She was staying on at the country club for another couple of days. The thought of what might happen between them in those two days made Anny's return to Paris the opposite extreme from the eager anticipation of the outward journey.

Van didn't come to Paris again for the rest of that year. He was never at Orengo when she went to see Bart. All her carefully thought out schemes to undermine his determination not to follow through came to nothing because he was never available for her to put them into practice.

His forecast that the publication of her profile of Aristide might lead to bigger things proved correct. Two French publishers approached her about writing a full-length biography and very soon she had an agent, a contract and an editor to advise her. Writing the book while keeping her day job meant cutting out almost all social life, but she continued to do the hospital-visiting which had replaced keeping an eye on the old man as her small contribution to the general good. Whenever she could spare an hour or two, she went to a children's hospital to read to and play with those who, for various reasons, had no one else to come and see them.

As Julie and Fran were going home for Christmas, and Anny wasn't able to get away for long, she persuaded Bart to come to Paris. Van, who was keeping in touch by E-mail, telephoned on Christmas Day. He was spending the holiday with Kate who was expecting a baby.

One comfort was that, when Anny asked if Emily was with them, he said, 'She always spends Christmas with James and Summer.'

When the all too brief call was over, Anny thought about that and decided that if Emily's attitude to Van was anything like her own, she would surely have fixed for him to join *her* relations. Or, if Van was mad about her, he would have made sure he was invited.

After Bart had returned to the Riviera, Anny caught a bad cold which, combined with some atrocious weather, made her long for the sunnier south. She had recovered from the cold but was still feeling under par when one of the children at the hospital died. He was a little boy of seven, of whom she'd become very fond. At the end there was nothing the doctors could do for him except take away the pain. Anny sat by his bed, holding his bony little hand, while his life flickered out.

She managed not to break down there and then, but when she got back to the apartment, which was empty because the other two were still away, she didn't have to control herself. She flung herself down on her bed and cried, mostly from grief for Pascal's short and lonely life—he had lost both parents as a baby and been raised by unloving relatives—and a little for her own aching longing to love and be loved.

The tears were drying on her cheeks and she was bracing herself to make the effort to get up and do something useful when the door bell buzzed. She blotted her eyes with a tissue and, not caring what she looked like, went to the door and looked through the little peep-hole Fran's boyfriend had insisted on putting in for them.

What she saw made her heart almost stop beating. Standing outside was Van. For a moment she thought about rushing to the bathroom to wash her face. Then he pressed the buzzer again and she was torn between trying to think of a reason why she couldn't let him in immediately and being afraid that if she didn't call out something he might think she was out and go away.

In the end she unfastened the chain and let him in. What did it matter if she wasn't looking her best? He was here. Nothing else was important.

'Why didn't you say you were coming?' she demanded, her voice croaky from crying.

He grinned. 'It wasn't a planned trip. I came on an impulse...' He noticed the state of her face. 'Hey, what's the matter? It's not Bart, is it? He isn't sick?'

'No, no...Bart's fine...or was when he left here. It's just something sad that has happened.'

'Tell me.' Van dumped his suitcase and his laptop case. He put his hands on her shoulders, looking down with such kindly concern that all her emotions bubbled up to the surface.

'Oh, Van...I'm so glad to see you...' she blurted shakily. Her face crumpling, she flung herself against his chest and, as he put his arms round her, burst into tears again.

What happened then was different from any of her imaginings. It began with Van hugging and comforting her, then drying her tears with his handkerchief before giving her a brotherly kiss on the forehead and then suddenly, with a deep groan, starting to kiss her the way he had once before.

From then on it was better than her most vivid daydreams. She kissed him back. His kisses became more passionate. He crushed her to him. She melted in willing surrender. Then he picked her up and carried her to the living-room sofa where they subsided together and went on rapturously kissing as if breathing had suddenly stopped being the way to stay alive and non-stop kisses were now the key to survival.

Eventually Van let her go, but only to strip off the raincoat he was wearing over his sweater and shirt. While he was at it he took the sweater off too. The time-clock had started the apartment's central heating and it was no longer chilly as it had been when she came home.

After they resumed their embrace it wasn't long before he began unbuttoning Anny's fine wool shirt. As he slipped a warm hand inside it, she knew with joyous relief that there was no going back now. They had gone beyond the point of no return and clearly he wanted to go on as much as she did.

They spent the night in her bed, not doing a great deal of sleeping.

Some time in the small hours, when she was lying with her head on his shoulder, he said quietly, 'I didn't mean this to happen until you were older. If you hadn't been crying when I got here, I'd have gone on trying to hold out…at least for another year. But once you were in my arms…once I'd kissed you…it was impossible. It's always been difficult…trying to act like a brother. Since the night of Kate's wedding, it's been worse. I kept remembering the way you felt in my arms. Staying away from you was a kind of slow torture.'

'But it's over now…we're together,' she murmured, snuggling closer.

After a pause, he said, 'I still wish you weren't so young.'

'Time will cure that, as Bart says. All that matters to me is that now I can tell you I love you instead of keeping it secret.'

In the morning, waking up first, Anny lay propped on one elbow, looking with pleasure and gratitude at her first and forever lover. She couldn't believe that anyone but Van could have taken a virgin and made her into a

woman with such tenderness and understanding of what
her body needed to carry it through that transition with
a minimum of discomfort and the maximum sensual
delight.

She thought the nicest way to wake him was by making love to him in the way described in the French manu-
al of love Bart had given her long ago.

Van didn't wake up at once but he smiled in his sleep
and his body responded to her touch even while his mind
was dormant. He came awake all at once and saw her
caressing him.

'Oh, God...I thought I was dreaming...but it's really
happening.'

He reached out with eager hands. Moments later it
was she who was lying on her back with him bending
over her, kissing her with a passion that was like a raging
inferno, consuming them both.

He had come to celebrate New Year with her. Until Fran
and Julie came back he stayed in the apartment. The day
they were due to return, he announced he had found a
top-floor studio flat in the Marais where they could set
up home together.

'Distance is dead,' he told her, when she thought he
might have to commute between Paris and America.

All through January it seemed to Anny amazing that,
if most people were making love on a regular basis, they
weren't all walking around smiling like Cheshire cats.
She felt as if she were in heaven because, at the end of
the day, Van would be waiting to make love to her before taking her out to dinner in one of the neighbourhood
restaurants.

For the time being her book was on hold. She hadn't
told him about it in case he insisted she worked on it
instead of spending every free moment with him.

That he hadn't asked her to marry him didn't bother

her. Marriage was only important if you wanted to have babies. As she didn't plan to do that until she was around thirty and had scaled all the peaks on her career-plan, marriage was for later, when they had both achieved what they wanted to do in their public lives.

Anny was naked except for a narrow gold bangle on her right wrist which she never took off. The outside had a simple design and the inside was engraved with their initials and the date of their first night together. Van had given it to her on her twentieth birthday. Now it was May, early summer, and they were relaxing in the gently swirling warm water of the vast pale green oval Jacuzzi, large enough for four or five people to wallow in it.

It was in their bathroom in a country hotel not far from the Château de Courson, thirty-five kilometres south of Paris. The château was the scene of an event called the Journées des Plantes which drew gardening enthusiasts from all over France and beyond.

Anny had been assigned to write a feature about it and Van had come with her because he was interested in the grounds of the château. They had been reclaimed from a state of considerable neglect twenty years earlier and were now an economic asset rather than a drain on the estate.

At the moment he had his eyes closed and she guessed he had decided to switch off for a few moments. It was something he did most days, preferably by stretching out on the floor, relaxing every part of his body and emptying his mind of all thought. If necessary he could do it almost anywhere. She had taken to doing it too, and found it incredibly refreshing and invigorating when the pace of life was hectic, calling for maximum energy.

She smiled at his withdrawn expression, admiring the muscular lines of his shoulders as he lay with his arms stretched out sideways along the rim of the bath.

When she judged it wouldn't be long before his eyes opened, she left her side of the bath, took a deep breath and submerged. There being no soap in the water yet, she could open her eyes and see him looking like a Michelangelo sculpture of an athlete at rest.

Between his long, outstretched legs his body was quiescent, but it wouldn't be in a few minutes' time, she thought, smiling to herself.

She moved towards him, her hands brushing lightly upwards from his knees to his hips. Almost instantly she felt his thigh muscles tighten, his mind return to alertness. Her lungs developed by years of underwater swimming, she had plenty of breath to spare. She put her lips to his skin, just above his navel, and trailed her mouth slowly upwards, pressing herself ever closer, feeling him tense. By the time she reached the top of his breast bone, his hands were gliding down her back and she could feel the expected response.

She drew back enough to look at him, knowing the softness of her breasts against him did the same thing for him as the hard wall of his chest did for her.

Van had the look in his eyes which always sent tremors through her and probably always would even when they had been together for years and years.

They kissed with the slow, sensuous pleasure of lovers who had explored every part of each other and, each time, become more accomplished in prolonging their mutual delight.

Without taking his mouth from hers, Van suddenly tightened his embrace and stood up, bringing her with him. He had to break off the kiss to reach for one of the enormous his and hers bath sheets the hotel provided. Lifting her onto the bathmat, he wrapped the big towel around her and reached for another for himself. While the bath sheet was mopping up most of the water on her body, Anny grabbed a smaller towel and, with impatient haste, rough-dried her hair. Then she discarded both towels and ran for the bedroom, with Van in hot pursuit.

Like boisterous children, they took a flying leap onto the king-size bed. As it gave under their weight, they were already reaching for each other. There was the usual brief playful tussle for supremacy which Van always won, unless he was in the mood to allow her to overpower him. This time it ended with Anny on her back, a willing prisoner with her captor looming over her, ready to take her but holding himself in check in order to prolong the ecstasy.

A long time later Anny gave a luxurious sigh. She loved this moment when, all passion spent, they lay quietly together, their heartbeats slowing down to normal, their bloodstreams ceasing to rush like white-water rapids, their breath no longer sounding like sprinters nearing the winning tape. If there was such a place as heaven, surely this must be what it was like. Somewhere totally carefree and peaceful where everyone had this wonderful sense of well-being, but all the time instead of, as here, on earth, only after making love and then only after making love to the person who held your heart. She couldn't believe that people who made love casually, without their hearts being involved, could experience the same deep satisfaction that heart-and-soul lovers did.

Lying with her arms round Van's neck, gazing into his blue eyes, so close that she could see her own reflection in his pupils, she said softly, 'I love you.'

He kissed her softly on the forehead before lifting himself on his forearms and easing his body away.

But when they had separated and Anny had turned on her side, Van curled himself round behind her and kissed the back of her neck, one of his hands enclosing one of her breasts as gently as if he were cradling a dove in his palm.

As she drifted into a light doze, she wondered why other people had so many problems with their love lives. The agony columns were full of cries for help from people who seemed unable to communicate with those supposedly closest to them. Between Van and herself there were no taboos, no inhibitions, no hang-ups.

At long last it had come right for them and she could see no reason why it shouldn't stay like this for ever.

That it might not always be plain sailing was signalled by the first major conflict between her job and their social life. In September Van, who was good at planning exciting surprises and giving her unexpected presents, most of them inexpensive but chosen with touching thoughtfulness, had arranged a weekend in Normandy, renowned for its superlative cuisine, to celebrate his thirtieth birthday. At the last moment Anny was obliged to stand in for a colleague who fell sick on the eve of covering a conference for leading businesswomen.

It was a chance for her to show she could handle a more complex assignment than any she'd dealt with before. But Van, although he didn't rage or sulk, was irritated.

It wasn't the only clash between her working and private life. That winter they happened with increasing frequency and sometimes they led to quarrels. But these always ended in passionate reconciliations.

When Project X was finally unveiled as Cyberscout, the first really user-friendly way of accessing the Internet, its success was immediate. Launch presentations at international computer shows demanded Van's presence since his was the driving force behind what the computer trade press unanimously described as a massive breakthrough which would bring more people online than any previous development in this area.

The night he came back to Paris, bushed but triumphant, Van asked Anny to marry him. She couldn't believe he had postponed his proposal until he was certain he was going to be extremely rich.

'How could you think it would matter to me? I would marry you if you were…an out-of-work road sweeper,' she told him, laughing.

Tired as he was, he made love to her. They fell asleep in each other's arms.

The next day it became apparent that getting married wasn't as straightforward as it had seemed the night before.

Van wanted to re-open the *palazzo* and start living there. He also wanted Anny to live there with him, all the time, not just whenever she was able to get away.

## CHAPTER EIGHT

THEY were still in vehement disagreement when they flew south for a weekend, Van to see the house, Anny to spend time with Bart.

One afternoon while she was sunbathing on deck, Bart went ashore and walked up to the house to find Van.

'You and Anny are having a difference of opinion, I hear. She's told me her side of it. What's yours?'

Van said, 'Haven't you already heard my side of it from her?'

'Women have a way of slanting things to suit themselves. So do men, come to that…politicians are experts at it. You tell me how you see the situation. Then I'll tell you what I think.'

From the loggia where they were standing they could see *Sea Dreams* at anchor and Anny lying on her stomach on a folding sun-bed, reading a book while her slim legs and bare back toasted.

Van said, 'I know you've never been happy about the way things stand now…our living together in Paris. I don't like it either. I love Anny. I want to marry her. I have a house and the funds to restore it and make it a fine home. We have everything going for us. The only obstacle is Anny's career. She speaks perfect French. I'm sure she could get a job on one of the papers within easy reach of Orengo. But she doesn't want that. Anything less than a national is too pedestrian for her.'

He paused, waiting to see if Bart was going to comment. When he didn't, Van went on, 'To be honest, I don't want a career-wife. A lot of guys can't afford to support a family. They need two people's input to finance the lifestyle they want. But that's not our situation. Restoring Orengo will be a long-term project needing close supervision. I think it would be more useful for Anny to take charge of that. She has all the right qualifications. She loves the place. She's artistic. She'll enjoy the research involved. She has a flair for getting along with people. At the end of the day she'll have something to show for her efforts. You know how it is with journalism: today's front page story is tomorrow's garbage-wrapping.'

'Journalism's in her blood,' Bart reminded him. 'Her great-grandfather was the editor of one of the best small-town papers in Britain, her grandfather was on *The Times*, her father trained as a print reporter and then transferred to television.'

He paused. 'We're all programmed by our genes. I reckon the reason I was drawn to the sea was because one of my grandfathers was a sea captain. Computers are relatively new but, if you were to look back through your family history, you'd find something to account for the way your mind works and the ambitions that drive you.'

'I'm sure you're right,' Van agreed. 'But most people are also programmed to mate and have children. I don't think Anny is the kind to be ruled by her head rather than her heart. I can't see her as a dedicated journalist with no time for personal relationships. Journalism has changed a lot since her grandfather's time. It's become pretty sleazy. Can you see Anny pushing and shoving her way to the front of the tabloid mob when they swarm round their latest victim? I can't.'

'The press has always had its squalid side. Even the senior professions, medicine and the law, aren't sleaze-free,' Bart said dryly. 'You can't decide Anny's future for her, Van. She has to work it out for herself. I understand how you feel. But the days when women were content to go wherever their man led are long gone, old son. Even thirty years ago, the one I wanted wasn't willing to break her ties with her family and come adventuring with me.'

'She may regret it now.'

'I shouldn't think so. It would have been a tough life for her...for any woman.'

'The life I'm offering Anny isn't a tough one. Very soon I'll be able to give her everything she's ever wanted.'

'What she wants at the moment is freedom and independence. You want to tie her down. I think you should try to be patient and let her find out for herself what's really important in life.'

'How long is that going to take?' was Van's grim-faced comment.

'Who knows? But it's no use going to the altar if she wants one thing and you want another. That's the route to the divorce court.'

Anny guessed that the two men had had what Bart called a confab but she didn't ask either of them what had been said.

To her relief, on the way back to Paris, Van stopped putting pressure on her. In the months that followed he didn't say any more about living at Orengo but nor did he mention marriage. It seemed that he had decided to let things go on as they were.

In March she was on an assignment in Lyons, making notes for an insight into the lives of the wives and daughters of one of the great silk manufacturing dynasties, when it struck her that her period was late.

Her cycle had never been erratic. After two days she began to feel alarmed. By the third day she was panicky. In theory there were all kinds of reasons why her insides might have seized up, but none of them seemed at all

likely, given that she had no health problems and was
not under any more stress than most people in her profession. She was forced to conclude that, somehow,
something had gone wrong and she was pregnant.

Instead of starting her article on the train back to
Paris, she sat staring out of the window, trying to come
to terms with the fact that, in a few months' time, she
might be starting to bulge.

She wanted a baby one day...but not in the foresee-
able future. Babies came later, much later, after she had
made her name as a journalist.

Van had timed a trip to the States to coincide with
her absence and wasn't due back till late that night. She
prowled the apartment, waiting for him to return. She
hadn't gone out to the airport to meet him because he
would see immediately that something was wrong and
she didn't want to tell him what it was until they were
alone together.

Having checked with the airport's enquiry desk that
his flight was on time, she switched on the TV and
checked all the channels, hoping to find a programme to
hold her attention for another hour. By ironic coinci-
dence, one of the characters in a long-running soap was
agonising over what to do about an unwanted baby.

Fran and Julie had been addicted to one of the soaps,
but Anny had never shared their interest. Now she found
herself identifying with the anxieties of the girl called
Isabelle, except that she was pregnant by a married man
who would ditch her as soon as he found out.

Annoyingly, Isabelle's dilemma was left unresolved
as the episode ended with the usual dramatic cliff-
hanger. It was followed by a quiz show. Anny switched
channels and forced herself to listen to a current affairs
discussion, but her thoughts kept wandering off.

At last she heard Van's key in the lock. She had
switched off the set and was already on her feet when

he opened the door. Dumping his overnight bag on the chair beside it, he closed the door and held out his arms to her.

'How was Lyons?'

'OK. How was your trip?'

Usually, when they had been apart for more than a few hours, she flew into his arms, her face alight with the joy of having him back. This time she walked, forcing herself to smile. Had there been any good news, she would have told him immediately. This news was better kept back until he'd had time to relax.

They kissed and he held her close. 'I missed you. What time did you get back?'

'About five. Are you hungry?'

'I ate on the plane. A shower's what I need...followed by a drink.'

He went off to unpack.

She had already rehearsed a dozen different ways to broach the matter on her mind. Opening a bottle of wine and a tin of olives, she wondered for the umpteenth time how he would react.

When Van joined her in the living room, he was wearing a white terry bathrobe and the pair of light tan deck shoes he wore around the house. The fluffy texture of the terry contrasted with the burnished sheen of the tanned skin showing in the V of the robe. He wasn't covered with thick hair like most of the dark-haired men to be seen on Mediterranean beaches. For her taste, he had exactly the right amount of body hair. But tonight the last thing on her mind was making love.

She poured him a glass of wine, placing a dish of olives beside it. But when he would have pulled her onto his lap, she deflected his arm and shook her head.

'I'd rather sit over here. There's something we have to discuss.'

'That sounds serious. What have you done? Run up a

massive debt?' He was smiling, expecting to hear something he would regard as trivial.

'I—I think I'm pregnant.'

Van's smile faded. There was a long pause before he said, 'How late are you?'

'Four days...but I've never been late before. Some people's cycles are never the same two months running. Mine are...always have been.'

'There's a first time for everything,' said Van. 'People who drink too much, or take chances, do have slip-ups. We're not like that. There's no way you can be pregnant. Wait a few days. It'll sort itself out.'

Although he spoke in the plural, it was he, by his own choice, who had taken the responsibility for that aspect of their life together. Early on, when they had discussed it, he had said that he didn't want her disturbing her system with chemicals.

At the time she had been touched by his protective concern for her. From what she had heard and read, his attitude wasn't the norm. But then Van was an unusual man who thought about everything more deeply and far-sightedly than the average person. She had trusted his judgement and his reliability. She knew that some of her colleagues wouldn't approve of a woman surrendering such an important responsibility to the man in her life. But they didn't know Van like she did...or had thought she did.

'If it doesn't sort itself out...what then?' she said, in a low voice.

'There is no "what then". You are definitely not pregnant, angel. If you were, there would be only one option. We'd get married and live happily ever after.'

His expression, as he quoted the last line of so many classic fairy tales, was that mixture of tenderness and amusement which normally she found irresistible. But tonight it was exasperating that he could smile and speak lightly of a contingency which, to her, was a disaster.

'How can you be so positive? No method is totally foolproof…never one hundred per cent safe.'

'It's usually the human factor which accounts for the tiny margin of unreliability,' Van answered dryly.

His unworried attitude riled her. 'And you of course are superhuman.'

She regretted the sarcastic comment the moment it was uttered, knowing it to be unfair. He was not a big-headed person who saw himself as flawless. Considering the brilliance of his mind, he was remarkably modest. She had heard him listening quietly to opinions she knew he thought asinine, but he never wounded other people's egos by demolishing their views in public. It had been unjust to accuse him of regarding himself as infallible.

Although she acknowledged this inwardly, she couldn't bring herself to apologise.

Ignoring her sarcasm, Van said quietly, 'You're tired and you've been bottling this up. Worries always seem worse when there's no one to share them. Tell me about the people you met in Lyons. Were they interesting?'

Usually she enjoyed talking over her assignments with him. Sometimes his comments added a dimension to her own observations. But tonight she wasn't in the mood to discuss anything but the feeling that her life was being swept off course like a boat which had lost its rudder.

'How can you sit there so calmly when a few months from now I may have to resign?' she exclaimed, her eyes stormy.

'That's nonsense, Anny,' he said calmly. 'There's no way you can be pregnant. Calm down and try to relax. It may be tension which is causing the problem. When people are stressed, they get all kinds of strange symptoms. If it hasn't come right in a few days, you should have a check-up.'

She knew what he said made sense, but it was easy for him to stay calm. It wasn't his life and his career plan which would be disrupted if something had gone wrong. One of the editorial secretaries was pregnant and for the past few weeks had been at the morning sickness stage. Anny had been in the ladies' washroom when Yvette had come rushing in, to emerge from a cubicle a few minutes later looking pale and groggy.

It didn't take her long to recover and carry on as normal. But Yvette's pregnancy was planned and she didn't intend to return after her maternity leave. It would mean making economies, but she planned to have two children close together and concentrate on them until the second reached school age.

It sounded like a sensible plan, but everything about Yvette's life was different from Anny's. She was eight years older and she wasn't climbing a career ladder. Like millions of married women, she worked because, although her husband had a good job, his income was swallowed by their mortgage and other essential expenses. Yvette's pay had covered the extras; holidays abroad, patio furniture, equipment for the coming baby.

To Anny, becoming a journalist was her basic reason for being. It came before all the other things life had to offer. She saw her twenties as her time for establishing herself professionally, not for being encumbered by a baby.

Van finished his glass of wine and poured another. He said, 'Let's go to bed. I've missed you.'

For the first time ever the suggestion repelled her. She lost her temper. 'I think you did this on purpose. I don't think it was a mistake. I think you did it deliberately.'

The desire she had seen in his eyes the moment before her outburst went out like a switched-off light. The planes of his face seemed to harden. He said quietly, 'With what object?'

She said hotly, 'The reason is perfectly obvious. You just said it yourself...there'll be only one option. With a baby on the way I shall have to marry you. I shall have to live at Orengo.'

Van rose from his chair. The muscles at his jaw were knotted under the taut brown skin. She had never seen him look so angry. But his voice remained under control. 'I'll sleep in the study.'

Her eyes still stormy, she watched him go to the door of the flat's second bedroom used mainly for work. But it did have a fold-up bed.

Without saying goodnight, he went in and closed the door. He hadn't denied her charge.

She spent a miserable night. As soon as she woke up next morning she knew Van had been right. She wasn't pregnant. She ought to have known it. Her bad temper last night, her impetuous accusation had been typical PMT. She was always touchy for twenty-four hours beforehand and her panic had made it worse.

When she went to tell him she was sorry, he wasn't there. He must have gone out very early. He was in when she came home that night and he listened to what she had to say and seemed to accept her apology. But this time they couldn't make peace in the usual way and the next time they made love it was on her initiative. Afterwards, she felt it hadn't completely healed the rift between them. In a moment of reckless anger, she had damaged their relationship and the only way to put it right was to give him what he most wanted. But she couldn't do that.

Two months later when, at least on the surface, their relationship was back to normal, Anny was head-hunted by the woman editor of one of England's national newspapers. It was an opportunity she hadn't expected so soon and she had to take it.

Van's reaction was, 'If you go to London, I shan't be going with you.'

'But it was you who told me "Distance is dead". If you can run things from Orengo, why can't you run them from London?'

It was rare for him to swear and when he did it had more impact than other people's casual expletives. He said, 'Because I don't bloody well want to. You've always known what Orengo means to me. If this flaming job is more important than I am, take it! You go your way and I'll go mine.'

'That's putting a gun to my head,' she flared back at him.

'You've got a gun to my head. If I want you, I've got to live your way. Well, I don't like your way, Anny. I want out of city life. I already have a house in a beautiful place and I want to live there...preferably with you but, if you won't come, without you.'

'Go ahead!' she retorted. 'I'm not ready to give up everything I've worked for to be your...your hand-maiden.'

'I'm not sure you ever will be.' His voice rasped with anger. 'You think you can have it all. You can't. Not if you want a man who isn't a wimp.'

Six weeks after their separation, she saw him once more, at her uncle's funeral. Bart's body was found in the sea but an autopsy showed he had died of a massive stroke, probably while climbing aboard from the dinghy.

The funeral took place at the Nice crematorium. Afterwards Van helped Anny to sail *Sea Dreams* out to sea and scatter the ashes. He was kind and supportive in practical ways during the time she was there. But she felt he had written her off and they could never recapture what they had once shared. She arranged for the boat to

be sold, taking a few mementoes of her uncle back to
London with her.

Anny had mourned the *contessa*. The loss of Bart
went much deeper. But her grief for him was nothing
compared to the agony of losing her best friend and her
lover.

Her unhappiness made her recognise the same con-
dition in other people. Previously, being young, healthy
and happy, she hadn't fully realised how much pain and
desolation was being suffered by people whose outward
appearance suggested prosperity and well-being.

Sometimes she saw more quiet anguish in the eyes of
matronly shoppers than in the faces of winos and beg-
gars. She could only guess at the cause, but she sensed
that, for whatever reason, they felt as she did. As if the
world had caved in on them. As if the future was a long
dark tunnel with not even a pinpoint of light at the end
of it. As if they were trapped in a freezer and were never
going to be let out.

Perhaps, from a journalistic point of view, it was useful to go through this; to learn from experience how
people felt when life knocked the stuffing out of them.

Many times, in those long sleepless nights which left
her feeling washed out, she wondered if she had made
the wrong choice, discarding something infinitely precious for something of lesser value.

Night after night she wondered if tomorrow would be
the day Van made contact with her. Surely he must be
as unhappy as she was? Surely he would change his
mind?

At first she had hoped that, as time passed, there
would be fewer reminders of him. But it didn't happen.
There was never a day when something didn't bring to
mind a remark he had made, a joke they had shared. She
had to stop eating chocolate because the taste conjured
up a vivid memory of her first kiss.

She had been working in London for three months, sharing a flat with Jill Carter, a fashion-page writer, when Jill's brother Jon came back from Holland.

Anny already knew a good deal about him. There were photographs of him and their parents in Jill's bedroom. When the doorbell rang on an evening when Jill was out, Anny looked through the peep-hole and recognised the man waiting to be admitted.

When she opened the door, he said, 'Hi! You must be Anny. I'm Jon.'

The day before she had interviewed a dog breeder. With his blond hair, burly build and friendly hazel eyes, Jon made her think of a golden retriever offering a friendly paw.

Finding out that she hadn't eaten and being hungry himself, he insisted on taking her out to the neighbourhood pizza parlour. Over supper, he did most of the talking, mainly about his work researching the Dutch bulb trade on a grant from a horticultural organisation.

Anny was always interested in other people's jobs. For a couple of hours, Jon provided a distraction from her personal problems.

Van was in America. He had spent the day in conference with his small group of associates. Already they were all rich men and steadily getting richer.

He had always been sure Cyberscout would be massively successful but now, because he'd lost Anny, it was a hollow triumph. Without her in his life, there was no real satisfaction in anything.

If she felt the same way—and how could she not after what they had shared?—surely it wouldn't be long before she changed her mind and came back to him?

It was easy for her to make contact. She knew his E-mail address. Several times a day and sometimes in the small hours of the night he checked to see if there was a message from her.

Wondering what she was doing, who she was with, if she was thinking about him, he sought escape from his thoughts on the Net.

Three months after the funeral and the day Anny and Van shook hands and went their separate ways, Emily Lancaster called her. 'I'm in London...flew in this morning. Are you free for dinner?'

Anny knew it would be wiser to say no, but was impelled to say yes. They arranged to meet at Emily's club. As soon as she had rung off, Anny knew she had made a mistake. An evening with Emily would send her right back to square one in her struggle to put the past firmly behind her.

Emily was waiting for her in the club's drawing room, the only other person there being an elderly man dozing in a deep armchair. She cast aside the magazine she had been reading, embracing Anny as warmly as if they had known each other all their lives.

'This place is fearfully old-fashioned but I hate staying in hotels,' she explained, on the way to the bar. 'I'm the great-great-niece of one of the founders so they give me preferential treatment. Not all the single bedrooms have their own bathrooms, but I always get one that does.'

While they had their pre-dinner drinks, she asked about Anny's job and talked about Cranmere, her forebears' estate. 'If you want a bolt-hole from London, you're welcome to use my flat there. Why not come down this weekend?'

For a moment Anny's heart leapt. Could Van be behind this invitation? Had he asked Emily to set up a meeting because he was starting to regret his intransigence?

She said cautiously, 'It's kind of you, Emily, but I'm not sure I'll be free. At this stage of my career, I have to be ready to go wherever I'm sent, often at very short notice.'

Emily looked at her thoughtfully for several moments before she said, 'I gather that was one of the reasons why you and Van decided to split. Is it working out…being on your own?'

Anny didn't know how to reply. She decided it was no use pussyfooting. 'Did Van ask you to check me out?'

Emily shook her head. 'He doesn't know I'm in London. We had dinner in New York a couple of weeks ago. He gave me the briefest possible résumé of the situation, then he clammed up and we spent the rest of the evening discussing the Net. Men don't talk about What Went Wrong the way women do. They can't verbalise their innermost feelings as easily as we can…although I would have thought Van was more in touch with his emotions than a lot of guys. Do you want to talk about it?'

'What did he tell you?'

'That you had different priorities. You want to concentrate on your career. He wants you to concentrate on him and Orengo. Is that a fair summary?'

'I guess so.' Anny looked out of the window at a terrace of tall Georgian houses across the street. 'How does our impasse strike you?' she asked, returning her gaze to the sympathetic face on the other side of the table.

Emily looked at the lighted candle casting its soft effulgence over the damask napery, the silver and crystal and the small bowl of anemones. She said reflectively, 'I've known and liked Van a long time and I felt an immediate rapport between you and me. I hope you did too. I empathise with *both* your points of view. When I think what it must have been like for women in the past, their lives controlled by men from the cradle to the grave, I'm thankful I wasn't born in an earlier era.'

She picked up her glass of the Chablis she had chosen to go with their trout. 'That said,' she went on, 'I know my life isn't as happy as it would be if I shared it with a man I loved...and also I know that wonderful men aren't thick on the ground. I can count the ones I've met on the fingers of one hand, and they all belonged to other women. So when, if ever, I meet the right man for me, I'll let him call the shots. Wherever he needs to be, I'll be right there with him...even if it's Antarctica or the Andaman Islands.'

A waiter came to remove their plates and ask what puddings they would like.

She waited until he had gone before she resumed the conversation. 'However...I'm a lot older than you are. For me, freedom has lost its savour. It's beginning to turn sour on me. So our perspectives are different.'

Without waiting for Anny to comment, she changed the subject.

She returned to it, briefly, when they parted. 'If you find you aren't needed this weekend, feel free to come...or any time when you fancy a spell in the country. Here's my card.'

A taxi, answering her wave, drew up outside the club's elegant portico. Emily opened the rear door.

Anny said, 'It's been a very nice evening. Thank you. Next time you must dine with me.'

'I'd like that.' Emily kissed her own fingertips, then pressed them lightly against Anny's cheek. 'Just remember that however much Van loves you, he's a man with all a man's needs. He's not going to live alone in that great house for ever. There will be a lot of women who would like to share it with him.'

'That cuts both ways,' said Anny. 'Women also have

needs and I'm working with men who are journalists too. They understand and sympathise if I have to break private engagements.'

Emily sighed and shook her head. 'Stalemate... deadlock...impasse!' she said resignedly. 'Anyway it was great to see you again.'

'For me too. Thanks again. Bye.' Anny gave her address to the driver and stepped into the taxi.

As it drew away from the kerb and swung in the tight U-turn for which London taxis were famous, she knew she should have been guided by her instinct to avoid tonight's meeting. Emily's final comment about Van had pierced her like a knife.

When she got back to the flat, Jill was out but Jon was there, replacing the flex on the iron which he had noticed was frayed.

Anny was glad to see him. She didn't want to be alone with her thoughts. She made him some coffee and they talked until Jill came home, an hour later.

Jon had known Anny for five months before he kissed her. It happened while they were spending Christmas with his parents. He and Jill had insisted Anny must join in the family festivities. Having nowhere else to go, she was glad to accept. Mr and Mrs Carter gave her a warm welcome.

On Christmas night, Jon gave her a playful kiss under a bunch of mistletoe. The next afternoon, on a walk, he kissed her more thoroughly. She submitted rather than responded, curious to find out what happened when another man kissed her. Several had made tentative passes but she had fended them off. She knew she wasn't ready for an affair. The idea repelled her. But Jon was different. He had become a friend, someone she could relax with, someone she trusted.

'I've wanted to do that for ages,' he said, still holding

her close. 'But I felt it might spoil things between us if I rushed my fences. I had this feeling there must have been someone in Paris…someone important to you.'

'There was…but it's over,' she told him. 'At this stage in my life I can't cope with heavy emotion. I hoped we could stay…just friends.'

To her surprise and relief, he said, 'OK, let's do that. Do you want to talk about what happened? Sometimes it helps to unbottle things.'

Anny didn't want to confide all the details, but she felt it was time to make clear to him the intimate nature of her previous relationship.

Mr and Mrs Carter had been married for thirty-eight years and had obviously instilled their own views in their children. Jon's eldest sister was married with three children. His other sister was engaged but not living with her fiancé. Compared with most of those Anny mixed with and interviewed, the whole Carter family seemed to exist in a time warp of values and customs discarded by trendier people.

She admired them for resisting ways they weren't comfortable with, but felt they would disapprove if they knew her background and especially her recent past.

'There's not much to tell. I was in love with someone who wanted me to give up my career and be a full-time wife. I wasn't ready to do that. He wasn't happy with the way we were…so we split.'

'I had the same sort of problem with my last girlfriend,' said Jon. 'She hated my being away so much. I could see her point of view. She wanted a guy who was around all the time. I used to write to her a lot but she hardly ever wrote back and I don't think what I wrote interested her much. When she told me she'd met someone else, it didn't break me up. I'd already realised we were heading for the rocks. But it sounds as if what happened with you was a lot more traumatic.'

'It was,' she admitted. 'I still haven't quite come to terms with it. I suppose I shall eventually. Other people do. Half the people I know are divorced or in second-time-around relationships. Journalism is one of the worst careers for breaking up marriages and partnerships. War correspondents have the highest divorce rate, but even feature writers lead more erratic lives than people in strictly nine-to-five occupations.'

When Anny returned to London, she still half-hoped to find a card from Van among those posted late or delayed. She hadn't sent one to him but, if she received one, she would respond with a Happy New Year card. There was no card from Van in the scatter of mail she and Jill found on their doormat. But there was one from Emily, a watercolour painting of Cranmere under snow. Inside, she had written, 'Your piece about being homeless at Christmas was brilliant. I'll show it to V in February. We're both bidden to join James and Summer at their ski lodge in Austria.'

This message, no doubt kindly meant, made Anny wonder if the Gardiners were matchmaking. She remembered Emily's remark about the paucity of wonderful men and how the few she had met belonged to other women. That no longer held true of Van and who could be better qualified than Emily, with her aristocratic background, to help him restore the *palazzo*? Also she had a far deeper understanding of his work than Anny, for whom a PC was simply the tool of her occupation. The complexities of programming, and the ethical aspects of the Net, were over her head.

The following autumn, she received another envelope with her name and address written in Emily's elegant hand. The panic she felt as she slit it open showed how vulnerable she still was. She could close her mind to Van, but his hold on her heart was as powerful as ever.

Unfolding the single sheet of paper, she was certain she was going to read that Emily and Van were going to be married. People often married on the rebound. Why shouldn't he?

Emily's news—that she was taking a year out to explore India—was a short-lived relief. Enclosed with the letter was a tear sheet from a glossy magazine: a page of photographs taken at a charity dinner in America. One was marked with an asterisk in the sepia ink Emily used for her letters. It showed half a dozen people in evening dress seated at a table. Four of them appeared to be listening to a speech. But one man's head was inclined to hear a murmured comment from the woman next to him. The caption listed their names. One sprang out from the rest as if the type had been bolded. 'Mr Giovanni Carlisle and his partner Ms Robina Maxton'.

Since Van kept a very low profile for a man whose company's rocketing profits made him the subject of widespread interest, Anny was surprised he had allowed himself to be photographed. Then she realised that the page hadn't been taken from a magazine available to the general public. It was from a prestige brochure put out by the charity. The captions of the other photographs included many well-known names. Van and his partner had been mingling with the sort of super-rich people charities needed to interest. She was sure he wouldn't have attended such a function off his own bat. Someone must have persuaded him. The woman in low-cut black velvet who was smiling as she whispered to him looked as if she would have considerable powers of persuasion.

Jon's time in Holland was over. Now he was working in Turkey.

Unlike his previous girl, Anny wrote to him regularly.

Letter-writing came easily to her and besides she missed his company, especially now that Jill had a serious boyfriend and spent every spare moment with him.

The next time Jon could afford to fly back for a long weekend, Anny went to the airport to meet him. He greeted her with the same affectionate hug he might have given his sisters had they been present. But after a kiss on her cheek, he then kissed her on the mouth in a most unbrotherly fashion. She knew, before he released her, that he had been patient a long time but now needed something more than friendly companionship from her.

As it happened Jill was away that weekend, visiting her boyfriend's family and hoping that when she came back there would be a ring on her finger.

At Jon's suggestion they had supper at an Indian restaurant round the corner from where he lived. Then they walked back to her place for coffee.

He was keen for her to write a story alerting gardeners to avoid buying the wild snowdrop bulbs from Georgia being sold by unscrupulous traders. Although sympathetic, Anny felt the story was of limited interest.

Over coffee they talked of other things. She had purposely avoided sharing the sofa with him, but even from a chair a rug's length from where he was sitting she was aware of the tension in him. Instinct told her he wanted to repeat the second kiss at the airport. She also knew it wasn't fair to keep him at arm's length for ever. She had two options. If she wanted to go on keeping her emotions in the freezer, she had to make that clear to him. Or she had to allow him to try to thaw her frozen heart.

Suddenly, Jon took the initiative. He got up from the sofa, came to where she was sitting and drew her up from the chair into his arms.

'Do you miss me when I'm away?' he asked quietly, holding her close, but without the possessive assurance of a man who took it for granted that a woman welcomed his embrace.

'Yes, I do…very much. You and Jill are my closest friends.'

'I want to be more than a friend, Anny,' he told her huskily.

She leaned her forehead against his shoulder, torn by contradictory emotions. Part of her longed for what he offered and part of her shrank from it.

Gently, Jon felt for her chin and turned her face up to his. 'I'd like to stay here tonight. Is that all right with you?'

She knew then that she wasn't ready, perhaps would never be ready.

Drawing away from him, she shook her head. 'I'm sorry…I'm very fond of you, but I don't…I can't…'

'It's all right. Don't worry about it. We'll just go on as we are.'

However deep his disappointment, he was too kind and unselfish to press her.

Later, when he had gone, she thought perhaps, if he had, she might have yielded. Sometimes, in the night, when she couldn't sleep, her hunger for love was almost unbearable.

Yet when Jon, whom she liked so much, offered her relief from frustration, she couldn't bring herself to accept it. Why was that? Not because there was any hope of Van coming back into her life. She had resigned herself to that. Yet still she couldn't break free from the feeling that, even after all this time, to make love with anyone else would be a violation. A betrayal of something so nebulous yet meaningful that she might not be able to live with the consequences.

# CHAPTER NINE

JON'S sterling qualities were never more clearly demonstrated than in the way he reverted, at least on the surface, to an uncomplicated friendship.

He was often away and sometimes when he was in London she was away. But when they were together, he seemed to enjoy their companionship as much as before. As for her own feelings, deliberately, she didn't spend time analysing them. Her life was extremely busy. There was little time for introspection. She concentrated on her career, channelling all her energy into her work which, like most dedicated effort, soon put her ahead of colleagues whose energies were diversified.

As the years passed, her assignments became increasingly interesting and high-powered until, when her contract ran out, she decided to go freelance. This would broaden her range even more.

Her success papered over the cracks in a life-structure which, deep down, she knew wasn't as sound as it looked to outsiders.

She suffered from nightmares and spells of depression. But she was determined not to succumb to the usual panaceas for stress—pills, cigarettes and booze—and instead turned to fitness routines and, when she could fit them in, courses to stretch her mind.

Sometimes, when an assignment took her abroad, she fitted in a few days' holiday. The longer escapes from everyday life to which other people looked forward were something Anny avoided, knowing that two weeks of sun, sea and sand, with warm starry nights, would not

only reanimate memories better forgotten but allow time
for introspection.

This was a state of mind she was careful to avoid,
concentrating on the fact that her life was going the way
she had planned it, the way she had chosen.

She had been based in London for five years when on
the same day two things happened to shatter the illusion
of contentment. One of them she had anticipated...but
that came *after* the thunderbolt of Greg assigning her to
interview the reclusive man known to the world as
Giovanni Carlisle.

As they walked back to Anny's flat, on the north side
of the park, Jon decided he couldn't wait till she came
back from France to know where he stood with her.

He had known from the outset that Anny was wedded
to her career. Whether now she was ready for marriage,
he wasn't sure. But he knew he was...more than ready.
He wanted to change his job for something more settled,
preferably in the country where the air was cleaner and
they could have a garden and start a family. But would
that appeal to Anny?

Despite her obvious preoccupation with tomorrow's
assignment, as soon as they reached her flat and had shed
their coats, he put his arms gently round her.

'Anny, you must know I love you...that I want to
marry you. I think about it all the time. I'm sure I can
make you happy...if you'll let me. Will you marry me,
darling?'

If he had asked her last night, or this morning, might
she have said yes? Anny wondered, meeting his anxious
eyes with a deeply troubled expression in her own.

What she felt for Jon came very close to love. It was
a good imitation. But it wasn't the genuine article. When
love was real it left no room in the heart for other loves,
except friendship and family feelings. She had tried to

love Jon. She had wanted desperately to love him and had felt she might be succeeding.

But since Greg's phone call, and the firestorm of emotion which had overwhelmed her when he said 'Because I've set up an interview with Giovanni Carlisle', she had known it was no use.

As long as the sight or sound of Van's name had the power to move her, she would never be able to give her heart to another man.

Gently, she freed herself from his loose embrace.

'I can't marry anyone, Jon. I hoped I could. I wanted to marry and have children and a family life. But it seems I'm going to have to settle for my career. I'm sorry: I shouldn't have done this to you. I should have told you at the start that I could only give you friendship.'

'That's not a bad basis for a marriage. Friendship lasts. Falling madly in love has a habit of wearing off.'

'If it's mostly infatuation, yes. But the real thing lasts for ever, no matter what. You're one of the most lovable people I've ever met. That's why I thought it would work. You are everything I like and admire in a man. But I can't give you total love, which is what you deserve.'

His crestfallen face filled her with self-reproach. How could she have done this to him? She should have known how it would end. Somewhere, deep down, she *had* known but, selfishly, had ignored it.

Jon didn't argue with her. After a pause, he said bleakly, 'It can only be because you're in love with someone else. It's this guy called Van, I suppose.' It was a statement rather than a question.

Anny was taken aback. How could he know about Van?

He answered her unspoken question. 'Ages ago Jill told me that when you were sleeping in the other bed in her room, while your room was being redecorated, you woke her up talking in your sleep. You were having a lot of bad dreams. The only word she could make out was "van". At first she couldn't understand why you were always dreaming about a van. Then she saw an American movie with someone called Van in it and the penny dropped.'

His mouth twisted in a wry smile. 'I thought by now you had got over him. I was deluding myself. I haven't taken his place. Even if you don't dream about him now, he's still there...the spectre at the feast. What happened? What broke it up?'

'My career broke it up,' she said flatly. 'I wanted to be another Martha Gellhorn. He wanted a full-time wife. There was no way to compromise. He wanted me fixed in one place and I needed to be wherever my editors sent me.'

'Where did he want you to be? Somewhere out in the sticks? What is he? A farmer?'

She shook her head, sensing that Jon's curiosity was akin to the strange compulsion to probe a painful tooth.

'It was long ago and far away. When I met you, I really believed I could make a fresh start,' she said sadly. 'Jon, I'm so terribly sorry. I never meant to hurt you.'

Hours later, when he had gone and she was packing her flight bag with the few things she would need, Anny wondered if Jon would recover from loving her. She hoped so. A love that didn't work out but refused to die was an affliction she wouldn't wish on anyone. But perhaps in Jon's case there was a woman somewhere who, in the years to come, would make him thank his stars that Anny Howard had refused him.

Life was such a strange business. If Van's parents had stayed together and if her parents hadn't died, his life and hers would have been different. He wouldn't have spent so much time at Orengo, she wouldn't have grown up on *Sea Dreams*: their paths might never have crossed. If she had never known him, she could have loved someone else. What she had never had, she would not have missed. Now, because for a time he had loved her, and she him, she was fated always to compare other men to him and always to find them wanting.

She slept badly and woke with a headache. Normally she loved travelling, even the parts that most people disliked such as sitting around in airports. Now that she was well-known and given carte blanche on expenses, she no longer flew tourist. The intervals between check-in and flight times were shorter and the waiting took place in more comfortable conditions.

At one time receiving the preferential treatment earned by her skill with words had given her a buzz. Taking taxis instead of buses or underground trains had made her feel special. She had revelled in all the perks, but most of all in the chance to meet famous people; captains of industry, statesmen, opera stars, outstanding athletes.

After a while, the excitement had begun to wear off. Today was the first time in months she had set out on an assignment feeling intense curiosity to find out what international fame and a business worth billions of dollars had done to the man who might, had things worked out differently, have been her husband.

When, driving the rented car, she reached the last bend in the road before the great gateway in the wall surrounding Orengo, Anny's mouth was dry with apprehension.

The wall itself gave the first indication that much had changed in her absence. It had been re-painted the colour she thought of as Mediterranean-pink. Unkempt overhanging creepers had been severely pruned, making them flower more profusely.

Even with peeling stucco and some of its finials missing, the gateway, surmounted by a bell in an ornamental arch, had always been impressive. Restored, it was even more imposing.

Anny parked the car close to the wall. As she approached the elaborate wrought-iron gates, no longer being eaten by rust, a man in uniform emerged from the lodge.

She spoke to him in Italian and had to show identification before he opened the gates for her. Clearly the days when an adventurous child could trespass here were long gone. Tight security prevailed.

She drove slowly down the sloping drive, taking in all the changes. It was in immaculate order with many new shrubs replacing those which had died from neglect. She saw more than one gardener at work and some comfortingly familiar glimpses of the ancient wistarias which for many years had grown up through the branches of tall dark cypresses and still adorned them with cascades of deep mauve flowers. But the place she remembered and loved had gone and could never be recaptured. Would its owner be equally changed?

A neatly dressed middle-aged woman was standing on the steps of the *palazzo* when Anny drove under the archway leading to the large courtyard at the rear of the building.

She introduced herself as Charlene Moore, Mr Carlisle's personal assistant.

'We were misinformed about your time of arrival, Miss Howard. We weren't expecting you until late afternoon. Mr Carlisle is out. He has kept tomorrow morning free for the interview. Tonight he is giving a dinner party at which you will meet some of his friends. Let me show you to your room. Benito will bring up your flight bag and garage the car.'

Anny was furious at finding her suspense extended. But she felt sure the mix-up wasn't the PA's fault. She looked efficiency personified.

Containing her irritation, Anny said, 'I was expecting to fly back to London tonight. I can manage without a nightdress but I can't attend a dinner party in this.' She indicated her suit.

'All the bedrooms are provided with overnight necessities for guests whose luggage has been mis-routed,' Charlene told her. 'I'm sure we can find you something to wear for the party.'

Like the grounds, the interior of the house looked very different from Anny's memories of it. Richly coloured Oriental rugs and runners muffled their footsteps as they crossed the hall to the staircase. More rugs formed a pathway along the wide upstairs corridor. Fine paintings adorned the walls. Lavish arrangements of flowers in scale with the lofty ceilings and tall double doors stood on top of antique chests or on pedestals. The impression was one of sumptuous elegance. But this wasn't what Anny had visualised when she had dreamed of living here. This was how houses looked when professional interior decorators had been given a free rein to achieve their idea of perfection. The results were always subtly different—and, in her view, inferior—from a house which was the creation of generations of a family, or of one inspired amateur.

'Is Mrs Carlisle at home?' she asked. 'Perhaps I could talk to her?'

'Mrs Edward Carlisle, Mr Carlisle's mother, lives in Connecticut. Mr Carlisle isn't married.'

'Oh…I had heard that he is…or was thinking of marriage.'

'There have been many rumours, most without any

foundation.' His PA opened a doorway and waited for Anny to precede her. 'This bedroom has its own loggia with a view of the coast. I hope you'll be comfortable, Miss Howard. If there's anything you need, you have only to ask. I'll go look for something you can wear to the party.'

Left on her own, Anny cast a journalist's eye over the luxurious room. It had a painted ceiling, an antique Italian bed with tall gilded posts at head and foot, and curtains of coral felt with deep quilted hems. The adjoining bathroom had walls of dark rose-veined marble with taps in the form of rams' heads. Flasks of iridescent Roman glass shimmered in the alcoves at either end of the bath. There was no overhead shower fitting, but a hand-held spray allowed hair-washing. Not for the first time, Anny felt grateful that her thick fair hair, nowadays expertly cut every six weeks, did not need professional attention to look good on special occasions.

She unzipped her flight bag and began to arrange its contents on the writing table. A state-of-the-art laptop had replaced the one given to her by Van when she was in her teens. Her second most important gadget was a tape recorder, small enough for her subjects to forget it was there. Completing her equipment was a 35 millimetre single lens reflex camera.

She was leaning on the balustrade of the loggia, gazing at the view and wondering where *Sea Dreams* was now, when Miss Moore returned with an ankle-length black georgette skirt and a white silk blouse.

'I think these will fit you, Miss Howard.'

'Are they yours?'

'Yes, but you're welcome to borrow them.'

'That's very kind of you. Rather than hang about, waiting for Mr Carlisle to come back, I think I'll go to

Nice and look round the shops. Is my car where I left
it?'

'If not, it can soon be brought round.'

Driving to Nice, Anny couldn't help wondering if making her wait till tomorrow for the interview, and forcing
her to attend a smart dinner party in borrowed clothes,
was a game plan to put her at a disadvantage. Van hadn't
been that kind of person when she knew him, but money
and power changed people. Some rich men became ec-
centric to a point not far short of madness.

Although she was grateful for his PA's willingness to
help out, the blouse was not Anny's style. It was too
dressy for her to feel comfortable in it. She would have
to find another outfit and perhaps some outrageous junk
jewellery to raise the eyebrows of the other women
whose diamonds and pearls would be real.

Her shopping didn't take long. She went to a boutique
she remembered from the days when she could only gaze
at the chic displays in the window. This time she went
in, emerging half an hour later with several carriers.

This was in the part of town where smart shops alter-
nated with bars and pavement cafés used by locals as
well as tourists for watching the world go by. Anny
chose a café at a point where several streets met and a
mime artist was standing motionless, waiting for someone to throw a coin in the box at his feet.

She ordered tea with lemon and watched him go
through his thirty-second routine while half-listening to
two Frenchwomen in animated conversation at the table
next to hers. Then, as the mime artist froze, her attention
drifted to an elegant woman in the pavement café on the
far side of the *place*. The man sitting with her was Van.

To catch sight of him unexpectedly was as shocking
as yesterday's call from Greg. She felt as if all the air
had been sucked out of her lungs and her heart had
stopped pumping her blood. It felt as if all her vital func-

tions had suffered a power cut.

Still mesmerised by Van's face, she watched him nodding agreement with something the woman was saying. What was different about him? Something: but precisely what she wasn't sure yet. His body hadn't changed. He hadn't begun the gradual deterioration of men who ate too well and exercised little or not at all.

He had always been sparing with gestures, keeping his hands noticeably still, rarely if ever using them to emphasise what he was saying. More than anyone she had known, he had focussed on the person he was talking to, giving them his whole attention. She could see he was doing that now. When she looked more closely at his companion, Anny could understand why.

The woman was not a beauty but even from this distance she emanated charm and character. She looked to be in her forties, an age group when, in Anny's observation, women either began to worry about losing their looks or they bloomed as never before. Van's friend clearly belonged in the second category. She was dressed in a simple but extremely chic suit. Her skirt was a more discreet length than those of the girls sauntering by in tight minis or short swingy kilts. But none of them drew Van's gaze away from his friend's attractive face, Anny noticed. She found it painful to watch their absorption in each other.

Was this woman his mistress? Had he given up thinking of marriage, finding it more satisfactory to have a relationship with someone who didn't even share his house but was always available when he wanted her?

Forgetting her tea, Anny sat glowering angrily at the man she had come to interview. She knew what she felt was jealousy, an emotion she had always despised. But it wasn't the woman who inspired this bitter resentment. It was Van: for forcing her to come here, for still being compellingly attractive, for causing the break-up with

Jon which would always be on her conscience until she heard he had found someone worthier of him.

Presently the unknown woman glanced at her watch and stood up, her manner making it clear she was reluctant to leave. Van also rose, kissing the hand she gave him. He watched her walk away. Then he resumed his seat, the glass on the table beside him being half full of what looked like Pernod and water.

He was still there, making his drink last, when Anny paid her bill. She debated joining him, but decided against it. She needed more time to compose herself.

They came face to face an hour later, in the belvedere where they had met. But this time Anny wasn't talking to herself and he didn't take her by surprise. She heard his footsteps on the path while she was looking at the sea. She turned, her eyes masked by dark glasses, and was leaning her hips against the stone balustrade when he came into view.

'Welcome back to Orengo. How are you, Anny?' His words and his offered hand would have seemed friendly enough to anyone watching.

But he didn't smile and his eyes were as cold as the blue shadows in an ice cave.

'Good afternoon.' She spoke as if to a stranger, putting her hand into his with instinctive reluctance to touch him, even in this formal way.

Once, while they were living together and discussing a mutual acquaintance with a slithery handshake, Van had said he had to take care not to shake hands with women as forcefully as with men.

This time he forgot and she had to control a wince as her knuckle bones ground together under the pressure of his fingers. Strangely, the moment of pain reminded her of all the times when his touch had been exquisitely gentle.

In the past, when these same powerful fingers had caressed the most delicate parts of her body, they had done it with a tender sensitivity, the memory of which had often tormented her in the hundreds of lonely nights when her body had clamoured for release from the prison of unsatisfied longings.

Now she slammed the door in her mind through which a flock of unbidden memories had been about to surge.

'Having summoned me to your presence,' she said coldly, 'you might have had the courtesy to *be* here when I arrived.'

'You must blame your paper for that. Charlene's the most efficient PA I've ever had. Any glitch in the arrangements won't have been her fault.'

'Did they get it wrong that you asked specifically for me?'

'No, I fixed that myself in conversation with your editor.'

'Why?'

'I was curious to see how you'd turned out, Anny.' He then had the casual effrontery to reach out and take off her glasses, using both hands to tilt the side-pieces upwards so they wouldn't catch on her ears. 'The light isn't strong in here, with your back to the sea. I like to see people's eyes when I'm talking to them.'

Several angry retorts jostled for utterance. She managed to bite them all back. It was important to stay calm. She mustn't allow him to ruffle her.

'Weren't you equally curious?' he asked.

'Not particularly. My life is too busy to spend any time looking back.'

'I thought curiosity was a journalist's stock-in-trade? You used to be insatiably curious.'

'Professionally I still am.' Deciding to take the initiative, she said, 'This afternoon, as you weren't here, I

went back to Nice. While I was there I saw you in one
of the pavement cafés. Who was the woman with you?'

'Her name is Candace. She's American...the widow
of a much older Frenchman. When he died, she preferred
to stay here. She grew up in the States, but Nice is where
she feels most comfortable now.'

'Really? I feel the same way about Nice as Tobias
Smollett.'

'And how did he feel?' asked Van, still holding her
folded sunglasses and eyeing her with an expression she
couldn't interpret.

'He called it "a place where I leave nothing but the
air which I can possibly regret".'

'Is that how you feel about Orengo?'

The question slipped under her guard like the thrust
of an expert fencer.

She said coldly, 'The Orengo I knew has gone.
You've made it a showplace...somewhere I hardly recognise. Is Candace your mistress?'

To her surprise, he laughed. For a moment she caught
a glimpse of the Van she remembered from the time
before things began to go wrong for them.

'Is that professional or personal curiosity?' he asked.

'Strictly professional.'

'I never discuss my private life. You may ask me
about my work, my house and my garden. The rest is
off limits. If you were personally interested then I would
tell you. But you aren't.' The look he gave her was
mocking and faintly malicious.

'Without any personal details, a profile isn't worth
writing.'

'Then put in the details you know,' he said, with a
shrug. 'Tell your readers about our affair. Expose yourself for a change. Tell them *you* were my mistress. It
will make an interesting twist.'

Her eyes flashed. 'I was never your mistress. We lived

together as equals. You didn't keep me. I paid my own expenses...or as much as I could afford then.'

'How many men since then have you lived with as equals?'

Anny drew in an angry breath. 'That's not your business.'

'If you aren't prepared to be frank with someone who was once a close friend, why should I bare my soul for the gratification of people I don't know from Adam? Let's make a bargain. If you'll be open with me, I'll be open with you. An answer for an answer. Agreed?'

When he spoke of their past friendship, a curious pain shot through her. As they had when he first appeared, memories came crowding back and this time she couldn't control them or shut them out. They whirled round her mind like a neat pile of autumn leaves caught by a strong gust of wind and scattered everywhere.

Reluctantly, she said, 'I've been too busy building my career to have time for relationships. There's only been one other man.' She hesitated, half inclined to admit that it had been a friendship, not a love affair, but then changed her mind. 'Not much of a tally compared with yours, I expect.'

'That depends on the nature of your relationship. Is it serious?'

'It's over...it didn't work out.'

'For the same reason as last time? Did he want you to give up your career?'

'You said "an answer for an answer". I'm not going to be interrogated while you say nothing.'

'What do you want to know?'

'How many women there've been?' But even as she asked, she cringed inwardly, not wanting to hear the details of her successors.

'None who've mattered,' he told her coldly. 'As they say, once bitten, twice shy. This coast is littered with women whose husbands neglect or bore them. They're fairly boring too, but they serve their purpose.'

Was he speaking the truth? Did he really use women only to satisfy his physical needs? The idea repelled her. At the same time she found it more palatable than the thought of his having several passionate affairs.

'How disgusting!' Her lip curled. 'You might as well have sex with a prostitute if you only want an outlet for lust.'

'Lust being something you know nothing about, I suppose?' The look in his eyes reminded her of all the times they had come home after an evening out and stripped off their clothes in a mutual frenzy of desire.

She looked at him with disdain. 'I've never made love with anyone who was just a body to me.'

She wondered how he would react if he knew that, since leaving Paris, she had never made love with anyone, period. Probably he wouldn't believe it. Fidelity was an ethic which had gone out of style, at least among the movers and shakers, the people who set the trends and lived at the so-called cutting edge of society.

'You never used to be a liar, Anny.' As he said it, he was appraising her figure with a familiarity which brought a rush of colour to her face.

'What the hell do you mean?' she demanded furiously.

Her anger seemed to amuse him, but although his mouth curled, his eyes were still arctic. 'Let me put it more kindly,' he said, with cutting sarcasm. 'You loved me...remember? Passionately. Sometimes you wanted me so badly, you could hardly wait to get home and tear off your clothes.'

After so long apart, that he still had a telepathic insight into her mind was unnerving.

'Don't tell me you've ever lain down for anyone else as eagerly as you did for me. I shan't believe you.' The flash of his teeth was like a silent snarl. 'You want me now. Your thighs are beginning to tremble even before I've touched you. I could take you now, and you know it.'

She said, her voice quiet and controlled, unlike the turmoil inside her, 'If you lay a finger on me, I'll scream the place down.'

The icy gleam in his eyes had suddenly changed to the blue at the heart of a flame. She recognised that look. She had seen it uncountable times while lying on a bed with his long body rearing above her like a stallion pawing the air. In the past his exultant maleness had thrilled the primeval woman lurking inside her. Now it chilled her.

'No, you won't,' he said softly. 'You'll melt in my arms the same way you always did.'

He shot out a hand, grabbed her wrist and jerked her against him. For a moment, holding her pinioned, he gave her a chance to carry out her threat. When her eyes flashed with rage but her voice remained mute, he gave a harsh laugh. 'You see? Even though you hate my guts for forcing you to come here, you can't control your secret lust. You knew, as soon as I sent for you, that if I wanted, I could take you. The only thing you don't know is whether I would want to.'

'If you try it will be a rape.' Her voice shook with rage and terror.

But it wasn't the desperate fear of a woman about to be violated. She was afraid, but not of being physically hurt. What terrified her was something quite different.

'A rape is forcing a woman against her will,' he said softly, looking down at her flushed, furious face with the flush of arousal tinting the taut brown skin over his arrogant cheekbones and his blue eyes narrowed and glittering. 'Your will to resist evaporated when we were shaking hands. Do you think I don't know that?'

'Damn you, Van…let me go!' She struggled, knowing it was hopeless.

'All in good time.' His voice was almost caressing. 'But first we have an experiment to conduct.'

Keeping her trapped with one arm, he used his other hand to hold her face in position for a kiss which began with unexpected gentleness. But almost at once it changed to a savage demand. Anny gave a smothered moan of protest as, out of the ashes of five years' loneliness, all the remembered sensations burst into flame.

## CHAPTER TEN

WHEN at last the kiss ended, they glared at each other
like bitter adversaries, both made temporarily speechless
by the volcanic emotions the fusion of their mouths had
released.

Anny knew, because she had felt it, that Van was
aroused to a pitch where he might not care if a gardener
came by and heard them panting and gasping on the
floor of the belvedere.

He had spoken the truth when he said that, if he chose,
he could take her here and now.

She had neither the physical strength nor, even more
vital, the emotional strength to resist him. His kiss had
drained her of everything but an elemental need to feel
like a woman again, a female in the arms of a dominant
male. The decision was his. She knew that. The feminist
side of her brain despised her capitulation. But neither
side of her brain was in charge at the moment. Her
senses were in control...or, more accurately, out of control.

It was Van who recovered first. Releasing her, stepping back, he said huskily, 'I knew the result beforehand.
So did you. But what you still *don't* know is whether,
tonight, I'll take you to bed with me.' He raked back his
thick black hair, his expression derisive. 'Don't waste
your breath being outraged. Don't claim that you'd
rather die than spend the night in my arms. You'd enjoy
it as much as you always did, and you know it.' After
a momentary pause to let that sink in, he added, 'And
much as you'd like to chicken out and run away, you

won't do that. Because, if you did lose your nerve, you'd also lose an important scoop.'

As she was about to blaze back at him, they both heard footsteps approaching. A man in a dark suit and tie appeared, probably the butler.

Speaking English with an Italian accent, he said, 'I'm sorry to disturb you, sir. There's an urgent call from America. These are the details.' He handed his employer a notepad. 'They requested that you call them back as soon as possible.'

Van read the notes and nodded. To Anny, playing the courteous host, he said, 'Excuse me. We'll continue this conversation later.'

Presently, when she had recovered a little, she returned to the house by an indirect route and went up to her room, locking the door in case Van tried to walk in on her while she was making up her mind what to do.

For a long time she sat in the chair on the loggia, gazing along the familiar coastline, and knowing that really there was nothing to think about.

Years ago, as a teenager, with an imperfect grasp of the forces that shaped people's lives, she hadn't been able to understand why, when he knew it was bad for him, Bart couldn't give up drinking.

Now, having worked with people who shared his habit, and known or interviewed others who couldn't give up cigarettes, fattening foods, or drugs ranging from sleeping pills to cocaine, she knew more about addiction and the often unbreakable holds all these things had on people.

What she hadn't realised, but saw now with terrifying clarity, was that ever since leaving Paris she had been suffering from withdrawal. And also attempting to suppress and deny her craving.

What had happened in the belvedere had had the same

effect as a dieter succumbing to chocolate or a nicotine addict lighting a cigarette after long abstinence. With one cataclysmic kiss, Van had revived her need to have him make love to her.

She had no idea whether he had meant his threat to take her to bed. All she knew was that she wouldn't, couldn't resist him, if that was what he chose to do.

Deep down she had always belonged to him, and always would.

She couldn't believe that he still cared for her. But if, for some complex reason to do with revenge and punishment, he wanted to have her, if only for a single night, she wouldn't be able to say no and mean it.

Not that she would make it easy for him. But the final outcome was as inevitable as this evening's sunset and tomorrow's dawn.

Once, at the time of their separation, she had refused to do what he wanted and walked out on him. But it had been a hollow victory. She had won her independence at the cost of her happiness.

From a worldly point of view she was a success. In a few more years, if things continued to go well, she would be a role model for aspiring women journalists. A fat lot of comfort that was last thing at night when other, less ambitious women were going to bed with men who loved them.

Perhaps she had lost the chance to have that kind of shared life. She couldn't settle for what poor Jon had to offer, and although Van wanted her physically, she doubted if he would ever again make an emotional commitment. She had held his heart once, but rejected it. He wouldn't offer it again.

The next time she saw Van, she was on the terrace where drinks were going to be served. The butler had asked what she would like. Wanting to keep a clear head, she had requested a tall glass of iced mineral water.

'What's that? A gin and tonic?' Van appeared round the corner, looking even more distinguished than the first time she saw him in a white dinner jacket. He had always had an air of authority, but now it was more pronounced.

'Water,' she told him. 'Unlike some of my colleagues, I don't run on liquor.'

'I can see that. Women who knock back a lot of the hard stuff start showing it sooner than men do.' His eyes appraised her white piqué top teamed with a long black skirt with a slit to above the knee which showed only when she moved or crossed her legs. 'You always did dress very well. That, at least, hasn't changed.'

'Thank you.' Although she acknowledged the remark as if it were a compliment, she knew that the qualification gave it a double edge which was the reverse of flattering.

'This party tonight…is it a special occasion? Or do you do a lot of entertaining?'

'Very little compared with most people on this coast. In fact I'm regarded almost as a recluse.'

'You didn't give that impression this afternoon. You seemed to be greatly enjoying your American widow's society.'

'That sounds almost like jealousy, Anny. But jealousy is a possessive emotion and, as you made very clear the last time we were together, you have no desire to possess or to be possessed.'

'I hope you don't mean to spar with me in front of your guests. If you do, I shall leave the table.'

The smile that twisted his mouth was that of a torturer considering what refinements of pain he could inflict on his victim.

'But you won't leave the house,' he said softly. 'The price of that gesture would be too high, wouldn't it?'

She was tempted to dash the contents of her glass in his handsome, sadistic face, but she managed to restrain herself.

'I wouldn't count on it,' she said coldly.

Van laughed, knowing that he could. 'That sounds like the first car now. Will you excuse me?'

He left her to fume while he went through the house to greet the arriving guests.

With a different host, in a different place, it would have been a good party. His friends were obviously rich, the men assured and well-groomed, the women beautifully turned out and friendly towards her. She had been afraid that Van's riches might have changed his attitudes and values, making him cultivate people who saw everything in terms of status. But the friends who were here tonight were not of that ilk. These were people Bart would have liked.

Introducing her to them, Van mentioned her biography of Aristide, but it seemed that none of them had read it, or realised she was also a successful journalist. This didn't dent her self-esteem. She was realistic enough to know that only people on TV could claim to be household names. On the whole, print journos' by-lines didn't have a lot of impact, unless they'd been going for years, and her book about Aristide, although well-reviewed, hadn't been a major bestseller.

Predictably the food and the wines were first-class. After dinner, they moved from one terrace to another for coffee, liqueurs and hand-made chocolates.

The first person to leave, quite early, was the frail-looking General Foster. Before saying goodbye to his host, he came to where Anny had been standing, looking

at the moonlit sea, since detaching herself from a group
a few minutes earlier.

'When one reaches my advanced age there's always
the possibility that one is looking one's last on all things
lovely,' he said to her, taking it for granted that she
would know he was quoting from a poem by Walter de
la Mare.

'When we were introduced, I had one of the lapses of
memory elderly people suffer from. I didn't immediately
realise where I had seen you before. Although it's not
public knowledge yet, allow me to tell you that the man
you are going to marry is one of the most estimable
people it has been my pleasure to know. Perhaps even
you aren't aware of the extent of his kindnesses. I belong
to an organisation which assists elderly expatriates such
as myself should they fall on hard times. Mr Carlisle has
been extraordinarily generous in financing medical care
and, in two cases, repatriation. I also happen to know he
has given several very substantial endowments to French
charities.'

'General…what makes you think that Mr Carlisle and
I are…might be involved with each other in that way?'

'He told me so…but even without his disclosure, I
might have guessed it. When two people are deeply attached to one another, even before they inform their family and friends they tend to reveal their feelings. More
than once, during dinner, I noticed him looking at you,
and you looking at him, in a manner which confirmed
what he had already confided to me.'

'What and when did he confide in you?'

'A few months ago. He had left me alone in his library
to look through a portfolio of some very fine botanical
drawings he has collected. Among them was a watercolour drawing of a beautiful young woman…yourself.
When I asked who you were, he said, ''The painting
should not be in there. It belongs in another portfolio.''

And then, after some hesitation, he added, ''That is the girl I hope, eventually, will live here…as my wife.'' Seeing you together tonight, I gather it won't be too long before you announce your engagement?'

She couldn't think what to say.

Misinterpreting her silence, the old man patted her arm. 'You can rely on my discretion. If there are reasons why you are keeping it private for the time being, no one will hear it from me. I merely wanted to tell you how much I admire your future husband. To have won such a man's heart, you must have a character to match your lovely young face. I hope we shall meet again. Goodnight, Miss Howard,'

He turned away, speaking to some of the others on his way to take leave of Van.

The General's revelation left Anny feeling devastated. Could it be true that, as recently as he claimed, Van had still believed they would get back together? Where had the painting come from? She had never sat for a portrait. She could only surmise that it must have been painted from the photographs Emily had taken on the night of Kate's wedding. For Van to have had that done supported the premise that his real feelings towards her were very different from those he had displayed so far today.

The General's going did not break up the party. The rest of the guests were still there at midnight when Anny could stand the strain of being sociable no longer.

She made her way to where Van was deep in conversation with another man. When her approach made them pause, she said, 'I'm very tired and would like to go to bed. Will you excuse me?'

'By all means. Goodnight.'

The look he gave her was curiously impersonal. It was hard to believe the General had really noticed him watching her with the ardent gaze of a lover during dinner.

Yet there was no denying that, two or three times, while Van was attending to the animated chatter of the women on either side of him, she had stolen glances at him, perhaps with her heart in her eyes instead of masking feelings as she was now.

'Goodnight.' She gave a polite smile to the man with him. Not bothering to say goodnight to anyone else, she went up to her room.

For a long time she paced the bedroom, considering the situation, unable at first to see any resolution. She remembered Emily's half-resigned, half-exasperated exclamation outside her London club. 'Stalemate... deadlock...impasse!' And so it remained, unless...

As she realised that there could be only one way to break through the barricade of pride which was making Van appear contemptuous of her while she pretended to dislike him, Anny became impatient for the guests to leave.

It was obvious that if Van still loved her, he would never come to her room and force himself on her. Those threats had been made out of rage: the understandable feeling of a man confronting a woman who had rejected everything he had offered her.

It was she who must make the first move towards reconciliation.

As soon as the guests had gone and Van came upstairs to bed, she would go to his room and ask him about what the General had told her.

It was nearly one in the morning when the last guests departed. Anny waited for another fifteen minutes before leaving her room to go to what had once been the *contessa*'s bedroom and now, she assumed, was where Van slept. She had undressed, let down her hair and taken off her make-up. Now she was wearing a short nightgown bought in Nice and the terry robe and matching mules provided in the bathroom.

Her heart beating in nervous thumps, she went softly along the corridor to the door she had so often passed through in times gone by. There was no response to her knock. When, thinking he must be in the bathroom, she opened the door, there was no light on. She felt for the switch. In the flood of light she saw that it was indeed Van's bedroom. The bedclothes were turned down and there was a photograph of Kate and her husband with two small children and two older ones on top of a chest of drawers. She recognised the dust jacket of a novel by one of Van's favourite writers on top of a stack of new books on the night table. But where was the room's occupant?

She found him where she had guessed he might be, sitting in the moonlight by the swimming pool. There wasn't a breath of wind but the surface of the water was no longer glass-calm as it had been earlier in the day. He must have had a quick swim and now, like her, was wearing a robe and had rough-dried his wet dark hair with the towel flung down on the flagstones.

For once he did not get up as she walked towards him but remained lounging in the chair. His damp and dishevelled hair gave him a raffish air. Under a full moon his skin, now shadowed with stubble, looked even more darkly bronzed than by day. The shifting reflections from the water made his eyes gleam. There was a bottle of champagne and a half-empty glass at his elbow. She wondered if he had had too much to drink. She had seen him angry before, but never out of control. Tonight he looked wild and dangerous. From years ago came the echo of Julie's voice saying, 'If someone drove him too far, I think Van could become *very* uncivilised.'

'You said you were tired,' he said brusquely. 'What are you doing down here?'

'I thought you would come to my room. You said that was what you intended.'

'I changed my mind,' he said curtly. 'Go back to bed. I shan't disturb your sleep.'

'You've been disturbing my sleep almost every night since we separated, Van. When I told you I was tired, I didn't mean physically. What tires me is living a lie.'

She paused to take a deep breath before plunging on. 'I'm sick of pretending to myself that I can live without you. I can't. I shall never be able to. If you'll have me...I want to come back.'

The sinews at the angles of his jaw were visible knots of tension.

'Why do you want to come back?'

'Because I love you. You're part of me. According to General Foster, I'm still part of you. He says you have a painting of me and you told him it was the woman you expected to marry. Had he got that muddled...got it wrong?'

Van sprang to his feet and covered the distance between them in a couple of strides.

Grabbing her upper arms with fingers which felt like steel clamps, he glared down at her upturned face.

'I could wring your neck. It would give me great pleasure to throttle you! Do you realise how many years of happiness you've wasted? If you knew it was a mistake, why in God's name didn't you come back to me? Why did I have to drag you back here by force? Did you think that my feelings for you would evaporate as soon as you weren't there?'

In spite of his bruising grip, she didn't flinch or protest. She could see he was ferociously angry, his temper a hair's-breadth from snapping point.

'I lied to you this afternoon,' he said savagely. 'I told

you there'd been other women. There haven't. Five years is a long time for a man to be celibate. It must be hard for a monk. It was a bloody sight harder for me. But there was nothing I could do about it. The woman I wanted had walked out to marry a career.'

Then, like a hawser taking impossible strain, he lost his last shred of control. With a sound like the snarl of a tiger, he snatched her up in his arms and tossed her into the pool.

Briefly, Anny went under, but with her mouth closed and her breath held. Instead of coming up gasping and spluttering, she was able to yell some extremely rude words at him.

'Guttersnipe!' Van shouted back. And then, in a transformation as startling as his sudden rage, he began to laugh. Stripping off his robe and flinging it down beside the discarded towel, he leapt in to join her, causing a surge of water which almost swamped her.

As one powerful butterfly stroke brought him alongside, he said, 'That's better: being wet makes you look like my mermaid again.' Treading water, he hauled her against him.

Sometimes, in the past, they'd indulged in wild roughand-tumbles, although only because it was fun to play at resistance and conquest. This time she didn't resist but accepted the punitive kisses with joyful submissiveness.

A few minutes later, he propelled them both to the nearest steps and bundled her up them ahead of him, the thin nightgown clinging to her body like some exotic and transparent seaweed.

'You won't need that any more,' he said, stripping it off her. For some moments they gazed at each other, both breathing hard, both with bright drops of water spangling their naked bodies.

'Now I'm going to make up for all the nights when I wanted you and you weren't here,' he said huskily.

Much later, they had a hot shower together in one of the changing rooms. While they were towelling their hair, Van said, 'I'm sorry about this afternoon in the belvedere. I didn't intend to be such a swine to you. But you looked so damnably self-possessed and stand-offish that it drove me insane.'

'It doesn't matter. Everything you said was true. I did want you...as I do again now,' she told him, smiling.

They didn't want to go indoors. The night scents from the garden, the star-spangled mystery of the universe overhead and the calm, moonlit surface of the pool were all part of their joyous reunion. They took armfuls of thick bathing towels onto the loggia and spread them over the damp cushions of a luxuriously wide lounger where, not long ago, they had made frenzied love without stopping to dry themselves first.

Now they could take their time, rediscovering all the erotic pleasures of the past which somehow, after long abstinence, induced even greater rapture.

At the end, Anny wept with happiness as she lay in his arms and felt their hearts beating in unison.

She woke up to find herself cocooned in more of the thick soft white towels of the kind found only in the grandest hotels or the bathrooms of the ultra-rich.

She could tell by the position of the sun that it was very early. No breath of air stirred the surface of the pool. No footsteps or voices disturbed the peace of the garden. She could hear nothing, not even birdsong.

As she lay, listening to the silence, she remembered a TV interview with a distinguished musician in which he had said noise was an enemy of thought. Now, in a place where there were no intrusive noises, she understood how great a luxury silence had become in the big city world she had come from. As a child she had taken it for granted. As a woman she had lost it. But Van hadn't. For him, silence was an everyday pleasure.

Van...the memory of last night brought her to full alertness. She knew it had not been a dream. The fact that she was here was proof of that and anyway dreams were never like reality. There was always something missing, or something wrong, or they were cut short at a crucial moment.

Last night had not been a fantasy invented by her subconscious. It had been real. But where was the man who had shared it with her? Why had he left her to sleep here?

As she sat up, she saw the baskets. On the floor round the wide cushioned daybed where she was lying stood basket after basket of roses. They could only have come from the flower market in Nice and what they must have cost she couldn't imagine. Even the last time she was here—and that was years ago—an ordinary bouquet of roses had been quite expensive. Here, massed in the baskets, were the makings of hundreds of bouquets.

How deeply she must have been sleeping not to hear them being put in position. Had he done that himself, or only directed the operation? If the latter, how amazed his assistants must have been. Such extravagant gestures belonged to the *belle époque* at the start of the century, not to this down-to-earth end of it.

Anny unwrapped herself. Inside the cocoon she was naked. She draped one of the towels around herself like a sarong. While she was doing this she saw that, beyond the phalanx of roses, there were other flowers. Carnations had been laid on the floor in groups of three. It took her a moment or two to grasp that the stems formed arrows, and the arrows led out of the loggia and round the edge of the pool.

Her clothes and shoes had disappeared, but a pair of
rope-soled mules had been left at the edge of the loggia.
Wondering where the arrows would lead her, Anny
wished she had a comb and a mirror to sort out her
tousled hair.

Realising the changing rooms would have mirrors, but
wondering if they would be locked, she went to the door
of the women's room and tried the handle. It opened.
Within was a spacious changing area with handbasins,
showers and lavatories. On the counter surrounding the
immaculate basins stood a neat row of toiletries and a
tray holding a comb and various hair accessories visitors
might want to borrow. There were even two hairdryers.
If she had wanted to, she could have showered and blow-
dried her hair. But she was far too impatient to follow
the arrows to do more than the essentials. She couldn't
wait to join Van, wherever he was.

At the far end of the pool, the arrows didn't turn in
the direction of the house but led downhill, towards the
sea. Halfway down, on the belvedere terrace, she paused
to look over the balustrade. Yesterday the bay had been
empty, a distant ferry to Corsica the only shipping in
sight.

Now, a few hundred feet below her, a smaller vessel
lay at anchor. The sight of it made her gasp in astonished
recognition. What was *Sea Dreams* doing here?

She ran the rest of the way down. When she reached
the beach, the appetising aroma of frying ham was drift-
ing across the water from the schooner's galley.

She cupped her hands round her mouth. 'Ahoy *Sea
Dreams*!'

Almost at once Van came on deck. He was wearing
a pair of white shorts. His tanned shoulders gleamed in
the sunlight.

'Good morning. May I come aboard?' she called.

'If you haven't forgotten how to swim.'

She laughed and unfastened the towel, letting it fall at her feet. For a moment she spread wide her arms, delighting in the air on her body, the sun in her eyes, the tall figure watching her from the schooner.

Then she kicked off the espadrilles and stepped gingerly over the pebbles, giving a little mew as the cold water swirled round her ankles. Once she was swimming it felt warmer and by the time she reached the schooner it felt wonderful. She didn't make straight for the ladder but circled the hull, pretending to be inspecting it and to be unaware that Van was following her round, watching her move through the clear water.

'You see...I haven't forgotten.' She rolled over, swimming a lazy backstroke, smiling.

'I didn't think you would, but right now it's time to stop showing off that beautiful body and come and have breakfast.'

He was waiting at the top of the ladder, holding out a long terry robe when she stepped on deck. She slipped her arms in the sleeves and pulled it around her. Then Van turned her to face him and kissed her.

'When I woke up and found the roses...it was like that poem,' she murmured, when he released her mouth.

'What poem?' Van's voice was husky.

She snuggled against him. '"...and I will make thee beds of roses, and a thousand fragrant posies." What time did you have to get up to arrange my lovely awakening?'

'Not that early. I had to find something to do to stop myself waking you up before you were ready to wake.'

'If you had, I shouldn't have minded.'

Van put her gently away from him. 'I wanted to talk to you, Anny, and for that you needed to be rested. Sit down at the table and I'll bring you some coffee.'

Since her last sight of *Sea Dreams*, the schooner had

undergone a major refit. Taking in the details, Anny wondered what changes had been made between decks.

'Where did you find her?' she asked, when Van reappeared with a tray.

'I've had her a long time, but yesterday the guy who looks after her and crews for me took her up the coast and didn't come back until late. If things worked out for us, I wanted her to be a surprise for you.'

'If things worked out for us?' she queried.

'We'll come to that in a minute. I'm hungry.' Having unloaded the tray onto the table set for two, he returned to the galley.

Anny, whose usual breakfast was an apple and a carton of yogurt, suddenly found she was ravenous.

When Van put a plate of ham, eggs and fried banana in front of her, she couldn't wait to tuck in. There was also a napkin-lined basket of hot croissants from which she deduced that the galley now had a microwave.

They ate in silence fraught with questions. But the essential question had already been answered. Last night, in the pool pavilion, they had come together like two parts of a whole.

She had once interviewed an actress who had talked at length about Yin and Yang, the two complementary principles of Chinese philosophy whose interaction maintained the harmony of the universe and influenced everything in it.

Anny had listened and made notes while privately thinking it nonsense. Perhaps it wasn't. All these years while she and Van had been separated, she had never felt as she did now. There had always been something missing, some flaw, some subtle discordance. Now that feeling had gone.

When they had finished eating, Van rose to clear the table. When she would have helped him, he laid a restraining hand on her shoulder. 'No, sit tight. I'll do it. The washing up can wait. First things first.'

'Do you have a T-shirt I can borrow? Now the sun's stronger, this robe is beginning to feel hot.'

'Sure.' A few moments later he came to the main hatchway. 'Catch!' A bundle of white cotton flew through the air.

Anny shrugged off the robe and for a few seconds sat enjoying her nudity. Then the thought of all the people who had had their privacy invaded by the long-range lens of a press photographer's camera made her quickly put on the shirt which had the schooner's name printed in a small circle on the front of it.

'Aren't you afraid of being pried on by paparazzi?' she asked, when Van rejoined her.

He had two glasses in one hand, a bottle of champagne in the other. 'We're anchored too close in for anyone to focus on us from outside my boundary wall.'

'They could climb the wall.'

'Not without breaking electronic beams and alerting the security guards. We have some unpleasant surprises for unauthorised visitors, including two large guard dogs trained to terrify trespassers. They don't actually eat them, but they look as if they might.'

She watched his fingers deftly unfastening the wire cage over the cork. He peeled away the gold foil and eased the cork from the neck of the thick green bottle, releasing a wisp of vapour.

'Don't you hate having to live surrounded by security precautions?'

'Have you found them intrusive since you've been here?' He filled the glasses.

'Not except for having to prove my identity when I arrived yesterday. But if they had been in place in the *contessa*'s time, you and I would never have met.'

'I think we met too soon.' He handed her one of the

glasses. 'That was the root of our problems. From the time I found you talking to yourself in the belvedere to the time we split up, we were always at different stages of development. Had we met for the first time yesterday, it would have been a lot simpler.'

'But we wouldn't have ended the evening making love,' she said dryly. 'It was only because I *did* know you that I let you…overwhelm me. One can recognise attraction instantly, but love is something else. It depends on a whole lot more than sexual attraction.'

'I agree. But when I fell in love with you, you weren't ready for grown-up emotions. I should never have agreed to our living together in Paris. You were still trying your wings and I wanted to cage you. I wanted to bend you to my will. No one has the right to do that. A man and a woman can share some ambitions and dreams, but they need to keep their individuality and have goals of their own. I know that now. I didn't then. Or, if I knew it theoretically, I didn't apply it to us.'

He touched the rim of his glass to the side of hers. 'To getting it right this time.'

Without being quite sure what he meant, she echoed the toast and lifted the glass to her lips, feeling a slight effervescence tickle her nose as she took her first mouthful of the vintage champagne.

Having drunk some of his, Van put his glass on the table and took her free hand. 'Will you marry me, Anny…keeping your freedom to be yourself as well as being my wife? If you will, I swear I will never put obstacles in the way of your career. I love you and need you…on any terms you care to name. If we can't be together all the time, so be it. Any share of your life you can give me will be better than the misery of living without you.'

The passionate declaration made her eyes fill with tears.

'It was misery for me too. I thought it was over between us and I tried to stick my broken heart back together and convince myself I could learn to love someone else. But no one could ever match up to you.' Her voice cracked, the tears overflowed. 'Why am I crying when I'm happy for the first time in years?' Having no handkerchief, she wiped her eyes with her fingers.

Van removed the champagne glass from her other hand and drew her out of her chair and onto his lap. 'You haven't answered my question. Will you marry me?'

'Yes, please.' She gave a long, tremulous sigh and snuggled against him. A few moments later she chuckled.

Stroking her back, Van asked, 'What's the joke?'

'I was visualising Greg's reaction when I call him to tell him the interview is off…and why. He'll think I'm out of my head. He has no idea that I know you.'

'Why scrap the interview? Why not go ahead and do it? That's what you came for.'

'No, it isn't. I told myself that I didn't want to come here…that I was under pressure…jeopardising my career if I didn't. All that was self-deluding rubbish. I came because I needed to see you again…needed to be near you if only for a few hours.'

She sat up straight, turning to face him and putting her hands on the warm brown skin of his shoulders.

'You said you wanted to see how I had turned out? Was that the only reason?'

'You know it wasn't. I'd been keeping discreet tabs on you. When word reached me that you might be getting serious about a guy you were seeing, I had to use the only ace in my hand.'

'Why didn't you use it sooner?'

'You held the same card in your hand. I'd been waiting for you to use it. You were the one who broke up our relationship. For a long time I hoped you'd be the one to mend it. It was Emily who told me I was being a stiff-necked ass. She told me that, when she was a teenager, James and Summer were crazy about each other but held off from saying so. She quoted Shakespeare at me. Something Puck said in *A Midsummer Night's Dream*. "Lord, what fools these mortals be!"'

'I think Emily could be in love with you herself,' Anny said, looking troubled. 'I hope not. I wouldn't wish that sort of unhappiness on my worst enemy, and I liked her very much…when I wasn't being stupidly jealous of her.'

'Don't worry about Emily. She had a bad case of calf love but she recovered. Since then there's been no one serious. The right man for her will turn up sooner or later. She's not that old,' said Van.

His hands were under the T-shirt, caressing her waist and hips. 'Would you like to see what's been done to the cabins?'

An hour later, wearing a pair of shorts he had found for her, Anny climbed down the ladder into the dinghy and they went ashore.

Strolling up the steep paths with her hand in his, she discovered that Van had become a knowledgeable plantsman who now knew the botanical names of everything in the garden.

They were passing the ancient olive tree, said to be six hundred years old, when he said, 'I sense that you're not too happy with the way Orengo is now. You liked it better the way it used to be.'

'It's always a bit of a shock to find somewhere, or someone, you loved has changed since the last time you saw them. I thought you were different…and you are, but it's an improvement,' she teased him. 'As for the house and the garden, perhaps they're a little *too* perfect. What they need is some children running around and mussing things up a little.'

His fingers tightened on hers. 'Do you *really* want children? I don't want you to do anything because you feel it's required of you. If I can have you in my life, even if not all the time, that's enough for me. I've had years to think about this. It's clear to me now that the fundamentals of happiness are good health, satisfying work and someone to share life with. There's a lot you can add on, but all those things are a bonus, not the basic essentials.'

She lifted their linked hands and pressed her lips to the back of his for a moment.

'I don't think it's possible to love a man and not want to have a child by him. I've also spent hours and hours thinking. I wrote a profile of a famous violinist for his eightieth birthday. I won't ever meet a wiser, more tolerant person. At one point in our conversation, he quoted that bit in the Old Testament about "To every thing there is a season, and a time to every purpose under the heaven".' I wanted to make my name as a journalist, and that was right...at that time. Now I want to be a wife and mother. If I can keep my career ticking over until the children are school age or even college age— fine. If I can't, I shan't feel frustrated. Maybe I'll change tack...become a different kind of writer. I might write the history of Orengo and some of the other great gardens along the Riviera.'

By a different route from the one she had run down earlier, they had come to the steps leading up to the belvedere on the opposite side from the terrace. The sides of the steps had been planted with tumbling nasturtiums and, behind them, great clumps of strelitzias, their flowers rising from their big leaves like long-necked birds with jade beaks and orange crests.

'I used to sit here alone, wishing I had you with me.'
Van released her hand to put his arm round her waist
and draw her close to him. 'Must you go back to
London? Can't we get married right away? We've only
just got back together. It's too soon to say goodbye.'

'We've said so many goodbyes and I always pretended not to mind, but I minded terribly inside,' she
confessed.

'So did I. You'll never know how hard it was to behave like an older brother while you were growing
up…that time in Minorca when you asked me to make
love to you. Bart would have torn me apart.'

'I still can't quite believe it's come right for us. It's
taken such a long time. What a fool I was ever to leave
you.'

'Let's put all that behind us. It's not important any
more. We can't change the past, or erase our mistakes.
The here and now is what matters.'

She looked up into his eyes which, when they had
stood here yesterday, had not held the tender ardour she
saw in them now.

For a moment she glimpsed the future they would
make together, foreseeing their happy family life at
Orengo and on board *Sea Dreams*.

Then Van bent his head to kiss her. The fleeting vision
faded. As he said, all that mattered was today, being here
in his arms and his heart where she belonged.

## Author's Note

*Long ago there was a real house called Palazzo Orengo on the Riviera dei Fiori, near the border with France.*

*In 1867, after many years in China buying silk for the European market, a Quaker merchant, Thomas Hanbury, spent a winter on the French Riviera, looking for a property. Eventually, from a boat, he saw the ruined Palazzo Orengo on a promontory on the Italian side of the frontier. He bought the land, demolished the ruin and built himself a palace to house his collection of Roman antiquities and oriental treasures. The new house was called La Mortola. For almost a century it remained in the hands of his descendants, becoming increasingly famous for the beauty and variety of the plants in the extensive garden.*

*Recently, in the spring, I visited some of the legendary gardens on the Côte d'Azur. They included La Mortola of which it has been said that passing through its gates is one of the great experiences of a garden lover's life, something they will never forget.*

*The house and its grounds are now in the care of the University of Genoa. The great garden is so large and labyrinthine that people can wander about and only catch distant glimpses of others there. My time there inspired the story you have been reading. Later, when I started to write it down, it seemed appropriate to borrow the name of the original building in that glorious location for the house where, in my imagination and, I hope, the minds of my readers, Van and Anny will raise their children and love one another for the rest of their lives.*

# HARLEQUIN ✦ PRESENTS®

**HARLEQUIN PRESENTS**
men you won't be able to resist
falling in love with...

**HARLEQUIN PRESENTS**
women who have feelings
just like your own...

**HARLEQUIN PRESENTS**
powerful passion in
exotic international settings...

**HARLEQUIN PRESENTS**
intense, dramatic stories that will keep you
turning to the very last page...

**HARLEQUIN PRESENTS**
The world's bestselling romance series!

# Harlequin® Historical

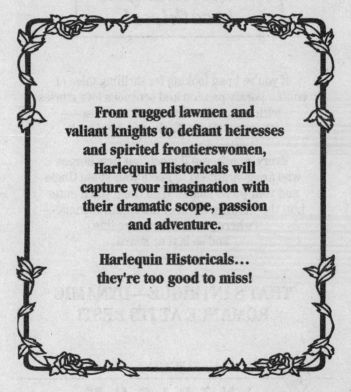

From rugged lawmen and
valiant knights to defiant heiresses
and spirited frontierswomen,
Harlequin Historicals will
capture your imagination with
their dramatic scope, passion
and adventure.

Harlequin Historicals...
they're too good to miss!

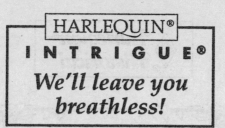

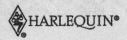

# Not The Same Old Story!

 Exciting, glamorous
romance stories that take
readers around the world.

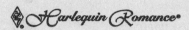 Sparkling, fresh and ten-
der love stories that
bring you pure romance.

 Bold and adventurous—
Temptation is strong women,
bad boys, great sex!

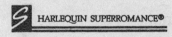 Provocative and realistic
stories that celebrate life
and love.

 Contemporary
fairy tales—where
anything is possible
and where dreams
come true.

 Heart-stopping, suspenseful
adventures that combine the
best of romance and mystery.

 Humorous and romantic stories
that capture the lighter side of
love.

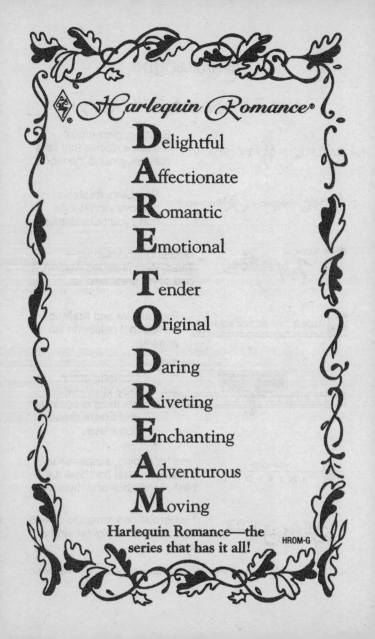

*Harlequin Romance*®

**D**elightful

**A**ffectionate

**R**omantic

**E**motional

**T**ender

**O**riginal

**D**aring

**R**iveting

**E**nchanting

**A**dventurous

**M**oving

Harlequin Romance—the
series that has it all!

HROM-G